"What do you want, Diana?"

Reece looked at her disbelievingly. "Do you want Chris—a boy of twenty, who can't even begin to match your inner maturity?" He shook his head. "I can't believe, knowing Chris as I do, that he can even begin to satisfy the needs of a woman like you."

She knew he was being deliberately insulting, and yet she felt the color drain from her cheeks anyway. "Needs...?" she repeated harshly. "I don't—"

"Oh, but I'm sure you do, Diana. I think you know exactly what I mean by needs."

D1021762

CAROLE MORTIMER, one of our most popular—and prolific—English authors, began writing in the Harlequin Presents series in 1979. She writes strong traditional romances with a distinctly modern appeal, and her winning way with characters and romantic plot twists has earned her an enthusiastic audience worldwide. Carole Mortimer lives on the Isle of Man with her family and menagerie of pets. She claims this busy household has helped to inspire her writing.

Books by Carole Mortimer

HARLEQUIN PRESENTS PLUS
1559—THE JILTED BRIDEGROOM
1583—PRIVATE LIVES
1607—MOTHER OF THE BRIDE

HARLEQUIN PRESENTS
1325—A CHRISTMAS AFFAIR
1451—MEMORIES OF THE PAST
1468—ROMANCE OF A LIFETIME
1543—SAVING GRACE

Don't miss any of our special offers. Write to us at the following address for information on our newest releases.

Harlequin Reader Service
P.O. Box 1397, Buffalo, NY 14240
Canadian address: P.O. Box 603,
Fort Erie, Ont. L2A 5X3

Carole Mortimer

Elusive Obsession

Harlequin Books

TORONTO • NEW YORK • LONDON
AMSTERDAM • PARIS • SYDNEY • HAMBURG
STOCKHOLM • ATHENS • TOKYO • MILAN
MADRID • WARSAW • BUDAPEST • AUCKLAND

If you purchased this book without a cover you should be aware that this book is stolen property. It was reported as "unsold and destroyed" to the publisher, and neither the author nor the publisher has received any payment for this "stripped book."

ISBN 0-373-11631-4

ELUSIVE OBSESSION

Copyright © 1992 by Carole Mortimer.

All rights reserved. Except for use in any review, the reproduction or utilization of this work in whole or in part in any form by any electronic, mechanical or other means, now known or hereafter invented, including xerography, photocopying and recording, or in any information storage or retrieval system, is forbidden without the written permission of the publisher, Harlequin Enterprises Limited, 225 Duncan Mill Road, Don Mills, Ontario, Canada M3B 3K9.

All characters in this book have no existence outside the imagination of the author and have no relation whatsoever to anyone bearing the same name or names. They are not even distantly inspired by any individual known or unknown to the author, and all incidents are pure invention.

This edition published by arrangement with Harlequin Enterprises B. V.

® and TM are trademarks of the publisher. Trademarks indicated with ® are registered in the United States Patent and Trademark Office, the Canadian Trade Marks Office and in other countries.

Printed in U.S.A.

PROLOGUE

'HAVE you just come here to gloat, Falcon?' her father's voice rasped disgustedly. 'Do you find some nefarious pleasure in watching your victims in their last death throes?'

She had been sleeping unobserved behind the curtains of the seated bay window in her father's study when the two men had entered the room a short time ago, had gone there to hide from Nanny and the lessons she had intended giving her. Having been sent home from boarding-school, because she had fallen victim to the outbreak of mumps that had stricken almost half the pupils of the school, it was completely unfair, she had thought, that she had to do lessons at home now that she felt a little better but was still contagious. There had to be some advantage to being sick, she had decided! And so she had hidden in the one place she knew Nanny would never think to look for her—her father's study—and then she had fallen asleep in the hot sun that shone through the huge window on this clear May day.

But she hadn't slept for long, her father's voice, raised in anger—something she had rarely known from the charmingly mild-mannered man during her nine years of life—easily intruding into her slumbers.

'You chose this way, Howard.' The man who answered her father's impassioned accusation spoke so
softly that she could barely hear him, and yet still she
could *feel* the power in his words.

'What other *choice* did you leave me?' her father
scorned with obvious contempt for the other man.
'You've taken it all, haven't you, Falcon? My business, my home, my—— My God, you couldn't even
leave me my pride, *couldn't* do that, could you? My
God, men like you make me sick!'

Whatever initial guilty thoughts she might have had
of revealing her presence behind the curtain had faded
almost as quickly as they came into her head; her father wouldn't like the idea of her eavesdropping—accidentally or otherwise—on what was obviously a very
private conversation, but from the little she had already heard she knew he would be even less pleased
now if she were to step out and reveal that she had
heard anything at all. She might only be nine years
old, but she knew this conversation was very serious
indeed.

Chalford, her home, the only one she had ever
known, gone? To this man, this *stranger*, a man she
couldn't even see properly?

She had tried to look at him around the edge of the
long wine-coloured velvet drapes, but she was too
frightened of being discovered to put her head out too
far. All she had was an impression of size and power—
oh, what power!—that seemed to emanate from his
very stillness.

He seemed to turn in her direction at that moment,
as if sensing he was being observed, and she quickly
ducked back behind the cover of the curtain, her

breath caught in her throat as she waited in terrified expectation for a hand to reach out and drag her from her hiding place to face the full force, not just of Nanny's displeasure at the way she had hidden from her so that she shouldn't do those awful lessons, but her father's wrath at her behaviour too. And his disappointment in her would be much harder to bear than Nanny's scolding...

But as the seconds ticked by on the grandfather clock that stood against one wall of her father's study, and no hand reached out for her, she slowly began to breathe again.

Once again the reply to her father's accusation was made quietly. 'No one twisted your arm, Howard,' the man dismissed calmly. 'You did it all yourself.'

'Oh, yes, of course I did,' her father scoffed scathingly. 'How easy it is for men like you to set traps for gullible men like me——'

'*Greedy* men like you,' he was corrected harshly, 'who blame everyone but themselves, the only real culprit, for their mistakes!'

She was filled with fury against this man. How dared he talk to her beloved father like that? She wanted to go out there and kick his shins for him, demand that he apologise to her father, who had to be the cleverest, most wonderful man in the world.

But before outrage could overcome good sense her father answered the man. 'The only mistake I ever made was in believing I could trust you!' he said self-disgustedly. 'Oh, get out, will you, Falcon?' He suddenly sounded very weary. 'Chalford isn't yours yet, not until the dust has settled and the lawyers say it is, and until that happens you aren't welcome in *my* home. Now get out, Falcon,' he repeated harshly. 'And take Janette with you.'

Janette? Why on earth would her stepmother want to leave with this hateful man, a man her father obviously hated? None of this made any sense to her.

'I don't want your wife, Howard,' the other man told him hardly. 'I never did.'

'Served her purpose, has she?' her father said with knowing contempt. 'Well, I don't want her any more either!'

'That's between the two of you,' the other man dismissed without emotion. 'I'm only interested in——'

'I know why you're here, Falcon,' her father cut in heatedly. 'And I've told you, you have everything else—the house you'll have to wait for. And much joy may it give you every time you think of how it came into your possession!' There was the sound of the door behind wrenched open. 'I've asked you to leave twice; if I have to do so again I'll call in the police and have you forcibly removed—I wonder how that would look in newsprint?'

There was silence for several long-drawn-out seconds after this direct challenge, and she suddenly realised she was holding her breath again, this time without even knowing she had been doing it. She didn't understand half the conversation she had unwittingly overheard, but she did recognise the raw emotion behind her father's words as he once again ordered the man Falcon to leave Chalford immediately.

'Very well,' the other man finally conceded, and there was the sound of him moving towards the door her father obviously still held open for him. 'I suggest we talk again, Howard, when you feel in a more reasonable frame of mind.'

'And *I* suggest,' her father returned tautly, 'that in future you stay well away from me and my family!'

The door was closed with only slightly repressed violence as the other man finally seemed to have left, and with his departure the room was suddenly filled with an ominous silence, a silence that seemed endless.

She wanted to run out into the room, put her arms around her father and tell him that she thought the Falcon man was hateful too, that she didn't want him to have her beloved Chalford, that he couldn't *let* that awful man come and live here! But if she did that she would give away her hiding place, reveal that she had been eavesdropping on their conversation. And, indulgent as her father was with her, she knew that would make him cross all over again.

No, she would just have to wait here now until her father left his study, and then creep quietly away herself. It was almost teatime, so she shouldn't have *too* long to wait, and her stomach rumbled hopefully; her father always joined them in the small family sitting-room for tea.

She could hear him moving about his study now, knew he had sat down at the desk, that he was opening and shutting the drawers as he looked for things he wanted. And then the room fell very silent, and as the minutes passed the muscles in her legs began to ache from the effort of having to sit completely still so that she wouldn't be detected.

Suddenly, when she was beginning to think she would have to move anyway and face the consequences, without any warning, except perhaps the smallest of clicking noises, the silence was shattered by a deafening roar.

For a moment she was just too stunned to move, and then her surprise at the sudden noise turned to puzzlement. She had recognised the sound only too well, often having accompanied her father on his seasonal 'shoots'. But he had always impressed on her, on those occasions, the importance of never having a loaded gun anywhere near the house, of always making sure the safety catch was on before handling a gun at all.

And yet she knew, without a doubt, that it was the sound of a gun being shot that had reverberated around the room seconds ago.

There was the sound of running feet in the hallway outside now, the door to the study being thrown open, the babble of the voices of the people who had entered the room—she guiltily recognised Nanny's as being one of them, and there was Sylvester the butler too, and Mrs Hall the housekeeper—coming to an abrupt and sudden end . . . possibly so that her father could reprimand them for entering his study without knocking, as they were supposed to do!

'My God . . . !' Sylvester finally groaned raggedly.

She wondered why Nanny hadn't rebuked him for the blasphemy, as she knew the elderly lady would have done if it had been her. The old lady had been Daddy's nanny first, was almost at retirement age now, and her old-fashioned morality lingered on with this, the second generation.

But her curiosity was now fast overtaking any fear she had of a reprimand for disappearing in the way she had after lunch, until finally she couldn't stand it any longer, silently leaving her hiding place, edging quietly into the room in the direction of her father's desk, which seemed to be where everyone else's attention was centred. So intent were they all that they didn't even see her.

What she saw when she reached the desk made her eyes widen with disbelieving horror, and all the colour drain from her cheeks. That—*that* couldn't be her father! It was too grotesque, horrific, unrecognisable as a human being, even. And the blood. Good God, there was blood everywhere. *Everywhere.* All over the pale blue shirt and checked jacket she knew her father had been wearing earlier in the day!

She opened her mouth to scream as she realised it *was* her father. But no sound passed her lips. And the silent scream went on and on and on . . .

CHAPTER ONE

'I'VE dressed some brides in my time, Di——' Joanna lovingly arranged the ivory-coloured veil for what must have been the dozenth time '—but you look— you look——' Words seemed to fail the twice-married and twice-divorced cynic.

'Fantastic!' Cally told her without hesitation as she burst into the room and heard the latter part of their conversation.

'Absolutely beautiful.' Joanna, perfectly capable of talking for herself, drily chose her own description. 'Of course, the gown could have something to do with it...!'

'It has everything to do with it.' Diana finally spoke from behind the sheer ivory-coloured veil with its beautifully arranged teardrop pearls draping her forehead. 'Charles is going to be delighted,' she said with husky confidence, squeezing the older woman's arms reassuringly.

'He had better be!' Joanna told her fiercely as she still fussed over the veil, seeking absolute perfection in its shimmering length that cascaded to the base of Diana's spine, her hair shimmering like gold beneath the whole length of it. 'I've had nightmares about the next few moments!'

'You had better get out there, Di,' Cally advised warningly. 'Before Charles is reduced to a quivering wreck!'

'And why shouldn't he be?' Joanna said with a certain amount of relish. 'After the week he's just given me, I feel like one!'

With a wryly affectionate smile for the older woman Diana glided over to the door in the ivory satin gown, the tiny teardrop pearls on her forehead the only adornment on both the veil and the gown, the simplistic lines of the latter outlining the perfection of her uptilted breasts, slender length of waist, and gently curving hips. It was a gown of sheer genius, a masterpiece.

'Oh, my God, I almost forgot to tell you in the excitement!' Cally hurried over to her, stunningly beautiful herself in a shimmering gold gown. 'The mystery guest has at last arrived,' she told Diana breathlessly. 'It's Reece Falcon!' The announcement was made with a triumphant note for the effect the man's identity was sure to have.

But Cally couldn't know just how much of an effect it had had on the woman so thankfully hidden behind the shimmering veil. Her cheeks paled, green eyes glazed with forbidden memories, her mouth suddenly dry.

'He's Chris's father,' Cally encouraged as she received no obvious response from Diana. 'Christopher Falcon,' she enlarged frustratedly as she still had no reply. 'The man who has been sending you red roses all week and generally making a pest of himself!'

Diana swallowed hard, fighting to regain control. It had just been the shock, the suddenness—— She had known she would have to face him again one day, but she had hoped it would be by her design, not like this, not today; she hadn't even realised he had been sent an invitation. But perhaps he hadn't, not in the normal way; Charles would have been sure to tell her of such an important guest. No, Reece Falcon had arranged this at the last minute; he was the sort of man who, when he decided he wanted something, made sure he got it. Getting himself invited here today would have been easy for a man like him.

Cally still looked deflated by her lack of reaction. 'Diana——'

'Will you stop delaying the girl?' Joanna cut in desperately. 'I can hear Charles building up to the finale now. God knows what he will do if Diana is late with her entrance——!'

'Heaven forbid the bride should be late,' Diana returned drily, fully in command of her emotions again now. Reece Falcon was just a man, with chinks in his arrogant armour like any other; hadn't she managed to find one of them? Wasn't that the reason he was here today? But there was nothing he could do to her, absolutely nothing he could do that would touch her either mentally or physically.

'There won't be a dry eye in the house,' Joanna predicted. Even cynically hardened as she was, she was obviously moved by the delicate perfection of the bride who stood before her.

Diana gave her a grateful smile before stepping proudly from the room, she could hear the expectant murmur of voices in the main room as she took her place in readiness for presenting herself to them, professionalism taking over as she stepped out on to the catwalk right on cue, barely aware of the awed gasps of admiration as she began her slow walk—just the way Charles had told her he wanted it done!—down the raised platform. Silence fell over the entire room as she did so, even the effervescent Charles, the designer-genius of the gown, having nothing further to say after he had announced the 'Divine Bride'.

All week, at this Paris fashion show, Diana had been showing Charles's 'Divine Collection' exclusively. For she *was* Divine.

It had all started out as a gimmick thought up by her agent and herself when she first took up modelling four years ago: the Divine Diana. But as her career took off she had simply become known as Divine to her colleagues and the public alike. This exclusive collection named after her was as much an accolade to her own success as it was to Charles's brilliance as a designer. This wedding gown, her final appearance for the week, was to be her—and obviously Charles's— *pièce de résistance*.

And from the stunned reaction of the audience, as they gazed up at her with wide-eyed wonder, it was having the desired effect.

But now, at this moment in time, Diana was interested in one reaction only to her appearance—that of the man seated in the chair in the centre of the row at the very end of the catwalk—a chair, placed between a beautiful redhead on one side and a lovely blonde on the other, that had, until a very short time ago, remained mockingly empty. Model after model, as they came backstage for another quick change, had exclaimed over this unusual fact as the show progressed. It was unheard of for a seat to remain empty in this way at the Paris Fashion Show. And right there, at the end of the catwalk, it had been so glaringly obvious to them all.

But the seat, as Cally had stated, was empty no longer, was now occupied by a man whose very size seemed to dwarf those around him.

It *was* him. Reece Falcon. Or just Falcon, as he was generally known. A bird of prey. How apt.

And Diana knew that today she was the focus of that narrowed silver gaze. Not admiringly, as with the rest of the audience, but with cold, raking assessment, chilling contempt stamped on every arrogant line of his harshly chiselled face.

The veil she wore acted as a shield, gauzy admittedly, but it nevertheless meant she could look out, while no one—including this silver-eyed devil—could look in. It was all the reprieve she needed after learning of his unexpected presence here today. She knew why he was here, of course, had known this moment would have to arrive eventually. That chink in his armour...

The photographs she had seen of him didn't in any way do him justice, could in no way tell of the power he emanated as he sat there so still and totally knowing. The lightweight hand-made suit he wore did nothing to tame the sheer animal savagery of the man, and neither did the cream silk shirt and neatly knotted tie at the base of his throat, all of them the trappings of civilisation worn by a man who lived by his own rules and not those dictated to him.

Dark hair that seemed inclined to curl was kept neatly cut to his perfectly shaped head, equally dark brows winging arrogantly over those narrowed silver-coloured eyes, the latter taking on a slightly luminous quality against the dark tan of his skin. His nose looked as if it might have been broken at some time in his life—probably by one of his many enemies, Diana dismissed with contempt—appearing almost hawk-like with that slight bump in its bridge, further enhancing his Falcon reputation, no doubt. His mouth was thin and unsmiling, his jaw square and challenging as his head tilted back in that steady assessment. A bird of prey, in fact.

But she had no intention of being his next victim!

As Charles had instructed, she glided to a halt at the end of the catwalk, pausing for effect, all eyes riveted on her now, before slowly raising slender silver-tipped fingers and lifting the veil back from her face.

As Charles had predicted, spontaneous applause filled the room as the full effect of her youthful beauty in the magnificently simple gown became apparent, several women openly crying at the simplistic perfection she presented.

Reece Falcon, Diana noticed, remained unsmiling, showing no emotion whatsoever, although that luminous glitter of his eyes seemed to have taken on a mesmerising quality.

Diana wasn't in the least conceited about the way she looked, had no illusions about her pale 'English Rose' beauty; after all, for the last four years her face and her body had been her fortune, and the photographers and designers left her in no doubt about the fact that she would only be popular for as long as those looks lasted.

Her golden hair, naturally wavy, reached to the base of her spine, framing a face that was hauntingly

lovely; green always-distant eyes flecked with gold
were surrounded by thick dark lashes, her nose was
short and straight, her lips full and sensual, her chin
small and pointed, her skin as pale and creamy as
magnolia. She had an almost Pre-Raphaelite beauty,
an unworldliness that made her much in demand both
for modelling and photographic sessions.

But she might as well have been a block of mis-
shapen wood for all the impression she had made on
Reece Falcon!

A cold lack of emotion remained in that silver-eyed
gaze as she moved first to one side of the T-shaped dais
and then the other to show the full effect of the gracefully flowing lines of the back of the gown, her hair
glistening like gold against the ivory veil.

Diana held her features composed in the dreamily
distant way Charles had wanted from her, her hands
steepled together almost in prayer as she walked, the
long ivory sleeves ending in a point that reached the
knuckle of the third finger of each hand. She had the
look of a proudly sacrificial bride.

The silence began to be broken now as some of the
women in the audience began to whisper together ex-
citedly, overcome by the majestic beauty.

Diana knew her composure must have slipped
slightly as the beautiful redhead sitting to the left of
Reece Falcon turned to him and murmured softly, the
blue-eyed gaze remaining fixed on Diana as she did so.

The woman had been here from the beginning of the
show, but when she laid a slender scarlet-tipped hand
on Reece Falcon's arm as she spoke to him, an act that
implied intimacy between them, it was obvious the two
of them knew each other very well.

It was the first indication Diana had had that Reece Falcon wasn't here alone.

It should mean nothing to her, *did* mean nothing, and yet—— Reece Falcon had had a string of women in his life since his divorce ten years ago, and it was unlikely this one would be any more significant than any of them had been, yet she hadn't realised he was involved with anyone at the moment...

Before she began that long slow walk back up the catwalk, to the sound of thunderous applause now, she found herself giving the other woman a more searching look. She wasn't as young as Diana had first thought; she looked to be in her mid to late thirties— very close to Reece Falcon's own age of thirty-nine— although the professionally artful use of make-up made her initially appear more youthful. Small and delicately made, and expensively dressed in designer-label clothes that Diana instantly recognised as such, the woman was obviously the sophisticated socialite Reece Falcon usually involved himself with. Beautiful as the woman was, she only held half of Reece Falcon's attention as she spoke to him, the other half being firmly fixed on Diana, and so she doubted the other woman would figure any more prominently in his life than any of those others had over the years.

Diana couldn't help the slightly contemptuous twist to her lips as she turned to begin the walk back, what-ever slight wavering of confidence she had momen-tarily known disappearing completely as those silver eyes continued to glare up at her; whatever place the beautiful redhead had in his life, she couldn't com-pletely divert his attention away from Diana!

The congratulations, once she reached the changing-room, from Joanna and the other models, passed over her head as if she was in a dream as she stepped out of the wedding gown to reveal that she wore only skin-coloured panties beneath, her breasts full and rosy-tipped, her body more slender unclothed than it had appeared in the exquisite clothes she had been modelling all week, her legs long and slim, each movement she made unknowingly graceful, her hair at last revealed in all its long shimmering glory as Joanna carefully removed the delicacy of the pure lace veil.

Diana's attention was held by the bouquet of roses that lay on a table in the corner of the room—today's offering from Chris, the card attached to them having remained unopened as they had arrived during the rush and bustle of the half an hour before the show began. She had felt no urgency to open the envelope and read the card inside because she had thought it would be the same as the others during the week; two simple words—'Marry me'. But perhaps this time she had been wrong; surely Chris knew his father was here, in Paris?

She hastily pulled on her robe over her near-nakedness, tying the belt securely about her waist even as she crossed the room to the roses, taking the card from the small white envelope and reading the message there. Those same two words still featured, but underneath, as if added later, was another message. It read, 'The Falcon is on the hunt.' They both knew the Falcon was his father. If only she had taken the time to read this card, she would at least have had some warning that Reece Falcon might be here in Paris, if nothing else. She had to accept that he probably knew something of her relationship with Chris too; the fact that he was here, tonight, was surely more than just a coincidence. It would more than explain that glitter-eyed look!

'Coming to the party?' Cally appeared at her side, unashamedly attempting to read the card that Diana slowly crushed in her hand, shrugging dismissively at the movement, the babble of voices continuing behind them, everyone obviously relieved that the evening had gone as well as it had and that the week of hard work was over.

With a tiny half-smile of apology, Diana shook her head in the negative. It had been a rhetorical question on Cally's part anyway; both of them already knew that she wouldn't go with the others to the huge party being thrown for them all.

'I thought not,' Cally grinned with an unoffended shrug. 'Back to the hotel,' she guessed, 'a good night's sleep. And then back to England on the first available flight in the morning,' she said knowingly.

Diana's smile widened at this totally correct assessment of her plans for the next twelve hours, the unguarded smile instantly revealing exactly how young she really was, the heavy make-up she had been wearing for modelling all evening tending to add years as well as the required sophistication.

'Am I so predictable?' She shook her head ruefully.

'I shouldn't worry about it,' Cally shrugged dismissively. 'It only adds to the elusiveness of the Divine Diana image.'

In part, it was only an image, one she had deliberately cultivated over the years. But the truth of the
matter was that she didn't really have any interest in
the social side of her profession; she earned her living
as a model, but she didn't feel that meant she had to
be on show the whole time.

And so she did her work, a professional to her
fingertips, always on time for assignments, never
subjecting the people she was working with or for to
moods or temper-tantrums, while at the same time
keeping her private life very private indeed. Which
wasn't as difficult as it sounded—not when she didn't
go out to the usual round of clubs and restaurants that
her colleagues frequented, and so gave the Press no
food for gossip. And people rarely connected the
young woman shopping in the local supermarket, or
walking in the park, with the glamorous model Divine
who often adorned their newspapers in one exotically
lovely gown or another. It seemed, with her glorious
cascade of hair confined at her nape or in a single plait
down the length of her spine, her face free of make-up,
and barely looking her twenty-one years, that she bore
no resemblance then to the beautiful model Divine.

She returned Cally's smile now. 'A good night's
sleep sounds a very welcome idea at the moment!' She
was thoroughly exhausted from the hectic pace of the
last week, and finding Reece Falcon sitting in the audience for her very last entrance of the week had been
much more traumatic on her nerves—and her energy
level—than she cared to admit.

But she went in search of Charles before leaving,
knowing he would be caught up in the crush of people who wanted to congratulate him on the success of

his designs; Charles enjoyed this adulation almost as much as he did putting the collection together in the first place.

Diana almost turned and left without talking to him at all when she saw *who* he was talking to; Reece Falcon!

Her desire for flight before she was seen was instinctive, self-protective—and, she decided with inner anger at herself, totally cowardly.

'Ah, Diana!' Charles smiled warmly as the congratulations she was receiving caught his attention, and he reached out a hand to draw her to his side, his arm moving about the slender width of her shoulders; he was several inches taller than Diana, for all her height. 'We were just talking about you,' he told her with satisfaction.

She tensed inwardly even as she compared the two men. The two were of a similar age, but Charles was tall, slender and blond, filled with a nervous energy that was evident in the way he found it difficult to stand still for any amount of time, constantly moving his hands as he talked, tapping those same hands rhythmically against his thighs when he wasn't. The other man, in sharp contrast, was very dark in colouring, and even taller than Charles, with a big, powerful body that nevertheless gave the impression of not having a superfluous ounce of flesh on its frame. And he was possessed of a stillness that was, in itself, more powerful than mere strength could ever be.

Diana assessed him coolly before turning her attention back to Charles; the flush of success was still on his cheeks. 'Oh, yes?' she prompted huskily.

'Not you exactly.' It was the other man who answered her softly spoken query—and at the sound of his voice Diana knew a sickening thud in the bottom of her stomach. 'We were discussing the wedding gown you modelled.'

She turned to him sharply, frowning. 'The wedding gown...?'

'Yes,' Charles confirmed slowly, although he looked at the other man somewhat quizzically. 'Although we hadn't quite got around to discussing your interest in it...?'

'I want it,' Reece Falcon stated with simple fact, never doubting for a moment that the gown would be his.

Diana still watched him with puzzled green eyes, not in the least surprised by his self-assurance that he would get what he wanted; this man always got what he wanted. What she was surprised about was what he actually wanted *this time*. The wedding gown. Why on earth——?

'Well, that's marvellous!' Charles told him with obvious pleasure, his arm falling away from Diana's shoulders in his enthusiasm. 'I had no idea!' He reached out and shook the other man's hand. 'I would be delighted to design a wedding gown for you—well, not for you personally, of course.' He gave a laugh at his own little joke.

Diana had no doubts as to the reason why Charles was so delighted at the prospect of designing a wedding gown exclusively for the Falcon family: the wedding gown would be photographed and shown all over the world, would earn its designer worldwide publicity and prestige.

But the fact that there was to be a wedding at all filled Diana with misgivings.

Silver clashed with green as she found her gaze meeting Reece Falcon's head-on for the first time, something akin to an electric shock passing through her body at the force she encountered there, a barely leashed energy behind the outward calm. He returned her gaze coldly, challengingly—almost as if he knew what she was thinking, feeling. Impossible. He couldn't *possibly* know!

The original Ice Maiden, Reece realised with mocking amusement. He had met many women in his life—too damned many, he acknowledged grimly—some of them, although not many, as coldly distant as this particular one. But none of them had been as young or possessed of such a removed air as this model Divine.

He was curious in spite of himself, and thought now that he should perhaps have taken the trouble to find out a little more about her before coming here, other than the fact that she was being disruptive to his plans for his son. Now that he had seen her for himself, and could see how beautiful but strangely elusive she was, he realised why Chris was so fascinated by the young woman that he had risked even Reece's anger to continue seeing her.

This young woman could be trouble with a capital T. Good God, there was no *could* about it!

He broke their gaze with easy dismissal, turning back to Charles Oxley, knowing a momentary satisfaction as he did so that the other man was no longer touching this exquisitely lovely creature—although he knew that none of that pleasure would be obvious in his expression; years of schooling his features and learning to hide his innermost thoughts and emotions meant that he now did it automatically. Until a few minutes ago when Diana joined them he had wondered at Oxley's sexual inclinations, but the way the other man looked at the model he was left in no doubt. Or was it just that this woman-child was so exotically lovely that no man could look at her without appreciating her understated sensuality...?

'I don't want a gown designed, Charles,' he drawled dismissively. 'I want the one I saw tonight.'

Charles frowned. 'The one...? But—I think the bride should see it first before making any decision, don't you?' he attempted to cajole. 'It may not be— what she wants for herself. I would be pleased to set a time when we can all get together to discuss what you would like,' he added lightly, obviously not wanting to offend by refusing the wedding gown Divine had modelled earlier.

Reece knew exactly why the other man was prevaricating, could appreciate Charles Oxley's reluctance to let a woman wear a gown, wedding or otherwise, that he wasn't absolutely positive would look right on her and at the same time be a credit to his undoubted reputation as a designer. At the same time that he could appreciate the other man's feelings, however, he also knew that he wanted the gown!

'She's seen it,' he told the other man drily. 'She likes it. It's what she wants.' And what that particular lady wanted, she got!

This time there was no mistaking a reaction in the model Divine as she stood at Charles Oxley's side. She didn't move, and her facial expression—strangely, for one so young—remained perfectly controlled. And yet Reece knew his words had disturbed her; he could feel the tension in her.

Tension was the very least of what this young woman should feel; she was responsible for trying to thwart his plans for Chris. A fact he intended rectifying at the first opportunity.

Although he had to admit, if Chris had to choose a woman to have a passionate fling with, he had better taste than Reece would have given him credit for. This young model Divine wasn't at all what he had been expecting when he'd heard of the relationship. Although she must only be a year or so older than Chris's twenty, at the same time she gave the impression that she was much older than that; there was also a vulnerability about her that he knew she tried to hide by her very elusiveness. A strange combination. Interesting. Intriguing... He already knew he meant to learn more about her.

He didn't question the fact that he found attractive the young girl his own son had told him he wanted to marry. Chris would get over the infatuation, hopefully learn from it, and there was little in Reece's own life that he denied himself once he had established in his own mind that he wanted it. And everyone, he had learnt with increasing cynicism, had their price. With Chris, this particular young lady's price appeared to have been marriage. But then, it was standard practice, in any deal, to ask for more than you actually expected to get. It was time Chris, as much as this young girl, learnt that!

'I'm flattered, Mr Falcon,' Charles began tentatively, 'that the bride should like that particular gown so much——'

'Don't be,' Reece drawled. 'This particular lady is used to getting what she wants.' Every time. And she was a beautiful, maddening bundle of provocation. He pitied—and envied—any man who tried to tame her.

Oxley still looked dismayed at the way the conversation was going, obviously searching for that narrow line between being polite to what he appreciated was a prestigious customer, and yet at the same time standing by his own professional reputation. 'But if we could just——'

'Charles—I'm sorry to interrupt.' A slightly breathless lady in her early forties bore determinedly down on them, looking at Reece briefly, chewing on her bottom lip as she recognised him instantly. 'Edgar Poole is looking for you,' she told Charles awkwardly.

Reece was well aware of who Edgar Poole was; he had done business with the successful entrepreneur several times in the past, and had actually gone into a couple of deals with him too. Successfully, of course. They both played to win. And Edgar's young and lovely wife would be the reason the other man was here at all today. Reece could appreciate Oxley's dilemma now in not knowing whether he should continue his conversation with him—one that he was finding it difficult to deal with—or go and see Edgar and the lovely Caryn, who might be more agreeable to deal with.

Reece decided, on this occasion, to take pity on him, inwardly admitting that he felt slightly distracted himself, but for quite a different reason. 'I'll give you a call within the next few days, Charles,' he drawled mockingly. 'But I won't change my mind about the wedding gown,' he warned him. 'And believe me,' he added derisively, 'neither will the bride!'

The bride. Every time she was mentioned Diana felt her nerves jangle. She had had no idea... In all the weeks she had known Chris, not once had he mentioned that his father was contemplating marriage. In fact, for years now, Reece Falcon had been avoiding that very state. Not that there hadn't been numerous women wanting to change his mind about that, but the man himself had just been determined he wasn't going to make that sort of commitment to any woman ever again.

But now that Diana was aware of the impending marriage she didn't doubt who the intended bride was to be; she had a vivid memory, as she walked down the catwalk in the wedding gown earlier, of a red-tipped hand resting proprietorially on Reece Falcon's arm as the beautiful redhead sitting beside him engaged him in conversation while her gaze remained firmly fixed on Diana wearing the gown.

From what Diana remembered about the other woman—and she wished now she had taken more notice of her!—Charles was right to feel concerned about the advisability of Reece Falcon's bride wearing that particular gown; the redhead had looked too short to be able to carry off the beautiful simplicity of the long flowing lines of the gown.

Diana found now, as she turned back to look at Reece Falcon as Charles hurried off with Joanna at his side, that her own gaze was on a level with the aquiline nose with that intriguing bump at its bridge. At the same time she also realised the two of them, for all that the room was crowded with people, were effectively alone. And now that she had learnt of his marriage she needed time to sit down and consider what effect that had on her own plans.

She gave him a politely dismissively smile. 'If you'll excuse me——'

'No,' he told her evenly, effortlessly.

Her lashes fluttered uncertainly as she looked at him, momentarily disconcerted. 'I'm sorry,' she finally shook her head. 'I——'

'Are you?' he rasped, eyes narrowed to silver slits.

She frowned now, unsure of the change of mood. 'I meant——'

'I know what you meant, Divine.' His mouth twisted with scorn for her professional name. 'I happen to think, having now met you, that you're probably enjoying yourself.'

Diana met his gaze unflinchingly. 'If I didn't enjoy my work, Mr Falcon, then I wouldn't do it any more.'

Dark brows rose mockingly. 'From what I hear of the fees top-class models—and I include you, obviously, in that category,' he drawled, acknowledging the slight inclination of her head, at the compliment, with one of his own, 'command nowadays, that would be a little foolish, don't you think?'

Her mouth firmed, eyes flashing slightly at the taunt. 'Some things are more important than money, Mr Falcon——' She broke off in stunned defence as he began to laugh at the comment, not a soft chuckle, but loud mocking laughter that had people all around the room turning to look at them curiously, a soft buzz of conversation instantly following as the two of them were recognised.

How dared he laugh at her? Just because he made money, and the power that money could buy him— power and money being the gods in his life—that was no reason to judge everyone else by the same cynicism.

He was shaking his head ruefully as the laughter died away, somehow appearing younger with his face relaxed in humour. 'Where on earth did Chris find you?' he mused disbelievingly.

She drew in a sharp breath as understanding dawned. 'Ah,' she nodded.

'Penny finally dropped, has it?' Reece Falcon taunted, his gaze sweeping over her disparagingly. 'You've been playing games with my son, Divine——'

'Diana,' she snapped irritably. 'My name is Diana,' she explained challengingly as he looked at her with raised brows.

'I thought Divine was a bloody silly name for any parent to have saddled a child with!' He shook his head self-derisively. 'But I take it Chris insists on calling you by it,' he added knowingly.

Chris thought her professional name was romantic. He also enjoyed being seen with someone as publicly known as Divine was. She had only been out with Chris to public places half a dozen times, but on a couple of those occasions they had been spotted together by the Press, and several questioning comments had appeared in the gossip columns concerning the two of them following that. It wasn't so surprising, then, that Reece Falcon had finally got to hear about their relationship—in fact, it was what she had been hoping for! She just wished she had had a little more warning...

'Chris is different,' she told his father huskily, meeting the narrowed silver gaze with steady challenge.

'Oh, yes,' Reece Falcon acknowledged sharply. 'He's very different. The main way in which he differs from other people is that he's *my* son——'

'We all have disadvantages in our lives, Mr Falcon,' Diana told him with contempt. 'It's just a question of trying to overcome them as best we can!'

For a moment he looked stunned by the quick viciousness of her attack, as if he very rarely came across such obvious antagonism directed towards him, and never from a woman. But as his initial surprise turned to deepening curiosity, his gaze searching now on the beauty of her face with its two bright spots of colour in otherwise pale cheeks indicating the anger she still felt, she knew that he found her outspoken attitude towards him intriguing in spite of himself.

'So it is,' he finally drawled appreciatively. 'But you must realise, Diana, that the two of us have to talk——'

'Not at all,' she dismissed firmly, half turning as if to leave, and almost gasping out loud as Reece Falcon's fingers clasped about her wrist to stop her from moving away. As it was she couldn't stop the way her eyes widened, or the way they shadowed to a deep emerald-green. 'Let go of my arm, Mr Falcon,' she instructed with careful control, her voice barely above a whisper now, although she knew by the way his gaze narrowed on her consideringly that he had heard every word she said. And he wasn't sure he wanted to do what she asked!

He shook his head finally, his fingers still like steel bands about her flesh. 'Not until you agree that we have to talk.'

Her breathing felt as if it were coming in short, painful gasps, she felt cold and shivery despite the heat of the room, and her skin seemed to burn where he touched her—and at that moment she knew she wanted to agree to anything to get him to release her. But ultimately she knew she wouldn't—couldn't do that; that she would never show any sign of weakness towards this man.

Instead she looked at him coldly. 'If you don't release my arm, Mr Falcon, I'm going to start screaming,' she told him with calm indifference. Inside she was just so relieved that she was managing to sound as controlled as she normally did—when in reality she really did feel like screaming! 'And when I scream it will be—— Thank you,' she accepted coolly as he slowly released her wrist as he saw she meant every word she said. 'The truth of the matter is, Mr Falcon,' she continued pleasantly, as if she hadn't just directly challenged the man—and won!—'that I'm very tired just now, and I actually intend going back to my hotel for a bath and a long sleep——'

'Which hotel?' he demanded quickly, his voice an

angry rasp, all his earlier amusement—at her expense—having faded.

'George the Fifth,' she supplied without hesitation,
having no reason to feel threatened; she had no intention of talking to this man *anywhere* tonight—she really did feel very tired after the gruelling week she had
just had. And talking to this man at all wasn't helping
her exhaustion; in fact her nerves felt stretched to
breaking-point. 'But——'

'Diana, you forgot to take these with you!' Cally
called out, hurrying over with the bouquet of red roses
Diana had left in the changing-room, and pausing to
give Reece Falcon an encouraging smile once she had
handed the flowers over to Diana, although she hastily made her excuses and left again when he just returned her gaze coldly.

Diana held on to the bouquet of roses. 'That wasn't
very kind,' she told Reece Falcon critically, knowing
she wouldn't really have expected anything else from
him!

'"Kind" isn't a word that I've heard often to describe me,' he acknowledged derisively. 'From my
son?' He looked at the roses with narrowed eyes.

Her arms tightened about the flowers defensively.
'Yes.'

He nodded, as if he had never doubted it. 'Then I'll
call at your hotel tomorrow morning and we can have
breakfast together. Unless——' his mouth twisted
mockingly '—you're one of those models who live on
lettuce leaves and black coffee?' He arched dark brows
questioningly.

She knew that some of her friends did have a problem keeping their weight down, although she thought a diet of lettuce leaves was probably a slight exaggeration; it didn't surprise her at all that Reece Falcon should be totally familiar with the problem some models had—no doubt he had been involved with more than one of them in the past!

'One of the things I've enjoyed most about being in Paris,' she drawled, 'has been my fresh croissants and creamy coffee for breakfast,' smoothly answering his derision.

He gave an acknowledging inclination of his head. 'In that case, I'll be at your hotel for breakfast at eight-thirty. Too early for you?' he challenged.

She shook her head coolly. 'Perfect.' Because by that time she would no longer be at the hotel but at the airport, waiting for her flight home!

'Tomorrow morning, then.' Reece Falcon nodded abruptly before striding confidently away.

Because he didn't doubt, as he had decided it would be so, that the two of them would be sitting down to breakfast together in the morning at eight-thirty!

Arrogant.

Self-centred.

Autocratic.

No wonder Chris found him just too much to try to live up to.

Well, if Reece Falcon thought that *she* was impressed by his arrogance he was sadly mistaken! Now that she had met the man, actually spoken to him, she disliked him even more intensely than she had before.

And she had already hated with vehemence the man who had ruined her father, made his life so unbearable that he had been left with no alternative but to take his own life...!

CHAPTER TWO

SHE was Divine.

International model. Travelled extensively. Was in demand for her unique brand of beauty all over the world. Always, as one of the highest paid models in the world, travelling first class, with champagne and roses—red roses, of course, her favourite flowers!—all the way.

Her suite at the George the Fifth was no exception—beautifully furnished with understated elegance, her bedroom dominated by the huge canopied bed she now lay in. But for all this quiet richness of her surroundings, and her own physical exhaustion, Diana lay wide-eyed and unable to sleep beneath the coolness of the bedclothes.

She wasn't even sure how she came to be back at the hotel at all; she vaguely remembered the comfort of the limousine Charles had arranged to be at her disposal during her stay in Paris, but nothing of her journey through the streets still crowded with people in the outdoor cafés and restaurants, and she certainly didn't remember entering the hotel itself and coming up to her suite.

Because of Reece Falcon...

She had been preparing herself for weeks for their first meeting. But when she had thought about it—and she had thought about it, often!—the meeting had always been by her own design, not sprung on her out of the blue as it had been earlier tonight.

It had shaken her much more than she could ever have imagined!

It had nothing to do with the way Reece Falcon looked—although God knew that was ominous enough. No, it had been the first sound of his voice again after all these years. She could have been blindfolded and would still have known the sound of that voice anywhere, was never likely to forget how the man had sounded who had forced her father to take his own life.

Because she wasn't just Divine. Wasn't just Diana Lamb, either. Her real name was Divinia Lambeth. Daughter of Howard Lambeth, a man Reece Falcon had taken delight in ruining.

She got restlessly out of the bed, giving up all idea of even trying to sleep, her cream silk nightshirt flowing smoothly over her body to mid-thigh, her legs long and golden beneath its length as she padded over to the window, gazing out over the beauty that was Paris by moonlight.

Not that she actually saw any of that, her thoughts too deep inside her as she cursed herself for not handling the meeting earlier this evening with Reece Falcon more calmly than she had. She had thought she could cope with it, had encouraged her friendship with Reece Falcon's son because she had believed that— and she had been reduced to a quivering wreck after only a single meeting with the man she had grown up hating with a vehemence she knew often bordered on obsession.

Not content with forcing her father into taking his own life rather than facing the public scandal her father knew would follow after revelations were made about his business affairs—although that had been more than enough reason for the young Divinia to hate him!—Reece Falcon was also responsible for destroying anything that might have been left after the loss of her father.

Everything they had had needed to be sold in an effort to pay off her father's creditors, and once Reece Falcon had claimed the family home as his own there hadn't been that much left to sell! But Divinia's life had changed irrevocably after her father's death, the indulgent childhood she had known wiped out in a single act. Her only consolation in all that had been that Janette had lost her extravagant lifestyle too. After what Divinia had heard during her father's conversation with Reece Falcon concerning her stepmother, she had felt the woman didn't deserve to have anything from her father anyway; she might have only been nine years old then, but she certainly hadn't been too young to realise that her stepmother had betrayed her father in some way. And with the passing of the years, her own maturity, she had been able to guess in what way Janette had been persuaded to betray her husband. The young Divinia had despised her beautiful stepmother almost as much as she hated Reece Falcon!

Which had been unfortunate, considering Janette had been made her sole guardian. And at nine Divinia hadn't been left with any choice but to do as Janette decided she should. But Janette had only been twenty-five herself at the death of her husband, and had certainly had no intention of being hampered with a nine-year-old stepdaughter now that she was on her own and there was no money for a nanny. Somehow Janette had managed to salvage enough money from the chaos to send Divinia back to her private school; it would have been kinder if she hadn't.

Everyone at the school, including Divinia's own friends, was aware of the way her father had died and the reason for it, and while a few of her really close friends had remained loyal a lot more chose to shun her; it had almost been as if her father's failure might rub off on them and taint them too. The following eight years of her school life had been miserable ones for her, and there was little respite from its overpowering presence in her life, as most of her school holidays were spent there too. Was it any wonder when she finally managed to escape from the place that she changed her name to Diana Lamb and tried to stamp out the misery of those years by severing all the ties she had with the people involved with them?

Janette had remarried within six months of Diana's father's death, to an Italian businessman who didn't give a damn about the scandal surrounding her first husband; he just wanted a beautiful woman—and there was no doubting Janette was still that, with her shoulder-length ash-blonde hair and deep blue eyes—that he could display socially on his arm when needed, and leave to her own devices when he found other diversions to amuse him. This arrangement suited Janette perfectly; her main loves in life were herself and the indulgences Marco's money could now buy her.

Whatever had been between Janette and Reece Falcon at the time of Diana's father's death seemed to have ended with Howard Lambeth's death, and Diana had been glad—*glad*: why should Janette find happiness with her father's murderer?

After Janette felt secure in her second marriage she had relented slightly in her attitude towards Diana, and allowed her to join them in their Italian home for several weeks of her school holidays throughout the year. Diana still despised her beautiful stepmother, but any time she spent away from the school had to be a bonus, and Marco was nice. Like a lot of Italian men, he liked children.

Unfortunately, however, Diana hadn't remained a child...

Her thoughts veered sharply away from that second distressing time in her young life. Reece Falcon. It was all his fault. All of it. If he hadn't pushed her father to the desperation of taking his own life, none of those things would have happened to her.

Which was why, since meeting Chris, she now wanted Reece Falcon to suffer the same pain she had.

Having now met the man himself, she knew that was going to be far from easy.

But she had to do it. *Had* to!

'All right, Puddle.' She chuckled softly at the antics of her cat, climbing up one of the legs of the yellow and pink leggings she wore in an effort to reach the bowl of food she was preparing for him. 'Lunch is served!' She put him out of his mewling misery by putting the bowl down on the cool tiled floor of her kitchen, watching indulgently as he launched himself into the bowl as if he hadn't been fed for a month.

Which was far from the truth. She had only been away for a week, and Roger, the man who lived in the flat across the hallway, and who looked after the cat while she was away, always told her Puddle ate enough for ten cats. Puddle, a pure black cat, with an elusively absent tail, always reacted the same to her going away: he seemed to sense when she was going and stopped eating for several days before she went, then gorged himself in her absence, and then ate everything in sight once she was back—including little nips out of her legs, just to let her know he didn't approve of her having gone away in the first place!

It was uncanny how the cat always knew she was going, even if she deliberately delayed packing until the very last moment. But after two years of being subjected to Puddle's unique form of protest Diana had decided it had to be the Celt in him that knew; he was one of those rare things nowadays—a truly Manx cat, totally bereft of a tail. He was also clever, intuitive, and didn't suffer fools gladly. He was the only companion Diana wanted in the large flat she had bought and decorated in her own particular style.

All the floors in the two-bedroomed flat, one of which she had made into a studio for the painting she did as a hobby, were either tiled or wood-panelled, with brightly coloured scatter-rugs thrown at random over their surfaces; the furniture, what there was of it, was all white, as were the walls. As Diana walked through from the kitchen with a mug of coffee, leaving Puddle to finish his brunch, she was like a bright splash of colour in the otherwise austere surroundings, wearing a bright yellow T-shirt over the garish multi-coloured leggings.

She dropped down on to one of the white bean-bags that lay about the room, relaxing back in its body-shaping comfort, letting all the tension of the day drain out of her as she sipped the strong coffee.

It had been an uneventful flight back from Paris early that morning, with very few people recognising the tall woman with her hair pulled back into a tight bun at her nape, wearing the white business suit and white blouse beneath the jacket, as the glamorous model Divine. It was exactly the way she liked it to be.

She enjoyed her work; she had really meant it when she had told Reece Falcon that if she didn't enjoy modelling any more then she wouldn't be doing it. She was thrilled that so many people liked the way she looked, how clothes looked on her. But that was the professional side of her life, and as Divine she accepted that, but as Diana Lamb she liked to keep her life very private indeed.

But even if anyone had recognised her on the early flight this morning they had been too polite to bother her. No, her tension had reached a head-pounding pitch long before she even reached the airport. She hadn't slept all night, had just been too tense, too haunted by memories, to be able even to think of relaxing enough to grab a few hours' sleep. Reece Falcon's presence in Paris had deeply disturbed her. As it was, she had packed and left the hotel long before she needed to, and had then sat around at the airport constantly looking over her shoulder in case Reece Falcon should already have realised she had gone and followed her there!

He hadn't, of course, but by the time she boarded the aircraft bound for Heathrow her tension had been such that she had almost leapt out of her seat when the air hostess approached her quietly from behind and asked if she would like a drink!

Lying back in this bean-bag, her eyes closed, the coffee-mug now hanging limply from her fingers, she realised this was the first time she had relaxed in over twelve hours. Since that meeting with Reece Falcon. She could almost, almost... fall asleep...

The strident ringing of the doorbell did little more than elicit a heartfelt groan of protest; she was too exhausted at that moment to do more than that.

She knew who it was, of course. Christopher had wanted to be with her in Paris this last week, but his father had sent him off on business for him—deliberately, Diana now realised—to America. Diana had told him how busy she was going to be with the show—too busy to spend much time with him really, and so he had finally gone to America, protesting all the way, hence the arrival of those red roses from him every day they were apart. But Chris should have arrived back in England this morning too, and had no doubt come to see her now with the intention of repeating his marriage proposal.

In spite of herself, she actually liked Chris. She certainly hadn't wanted to, having considered before she met him that as Reece Falcon's only child he was as much the enemy as his father was. But Chris was nothing like Reece Falcon; he was very easygoing by nature, and, taking after his American-born mother in looks, tall and blond, with the physique of an athlete. Even so, Diana had no intention of marrying him...!

'Keep my seat warm, Puddle,' she sighed wearily as she got up to answer the second ring of the doorbell, the now bulging cat instantly taking her place on the warm cushion.

But the tired smile of welcome that curved her lips froze into something resembling a grimace as she opened the door to find it wasn't Chris who stood there at all, but his father—Reece Falcon!

Silver eyes glittered with mocking satisfaction as he saw the stunned expression she was too tired to mask, his mouth twisting derisively. 'Breakfast.' He held up the brown paper carrier-bag he held in one arm. 'I told you we would have breakfast together.'

And what he 'told' her he was going to do, he obviously did, Diana realised dazedly as he brushed past her into the flat, easily finding his way into her spacious kitchen—probably following the smell of coffee!—the sound of his whistling coming from there seconds later, accompanied by the rustling of the paper bag as he obviously unpacked its contents.

She had seriously underestimated him over this, Diana now realised. She had thought that, once he discovered she had left the hotel before his arrival, he might just follow her to the airport; it had never occurred to her that he would follow her back to London!

But it *should* have done, she now berated herself. Who better than she to know how arrogantly single-minded this man could be when he set his mind to it?

By the time she followed him into the kitchen he had unpacked croissants, pastries and fruit into bowls and on to plates—a traditional French breakfast, in fact! This man didn't do anything by halves, Diana acknowledged; he had told her he would be joining her for breakfast, and a true continental breakfast it was going to be. It might almost have come from France itself. In fact—he might just have done exactly that. Chris had told her his father flew around the world in his own jet; there was no reason why he shouldn't have brought breakfast back from Paris with him this morning!

'Ah, coffee.' He picked up the pot Diana had made only minutes earlier, pouring them both a fresh mugful. 'It's good,' he told her appreciatively after the first sip.

Diana was still stunned into silence. This flat, with its simplicity of design, was her own private little haven. And this man had just invaded it without a qualm. Certainly without an invitation!

'Drink up,' he encouraged briskly as her mug of coffee remained untouched on the marble worktop. 'And we'll take the food through to the sitting-room.' He easily balanced the plates in the expansive strength of his hands. 'I had a brief glimpse of that room on the way in here; I'd like to have a closer look,' he added almost to himself, striding out of the kitchen with sure steps.

Once again Diana followed him dazedly, feeling as if she were following in the wake of a tidal wave!

He was dressed totally in black today, in a loose short-sleeved shirt with black fitted trousers that drew attention to the lean length of his legs. He looked every one of his thirty-nine years, lines of experience beside his eyes and mouth, and yet at the same time he possessed a dangerous magnetism that made age irrelevant.

'Puddle,' Diana finally managed to say weakly as Reece put the laden plates down on the rug in front of the bean-bags.

He looked up at her with raised brows. 'I beg your pardon?'

'The cat,' she explained a little impatiently, feeling as if she were being treated—and for the most part, acting, she freely admitted—like an idiot.

But once again his unexpected appearance had thrown her completely; it was the only excuse she could give herself for her lack of force, for allowing him to invade her home in the way he had. But her strength had always been of a different kind than force. It was only now, when faced with Reece Falcon himself, that she realised how ineffective that might be in dealing with him!

Gobsmacked.

Not very grammatical. Certainly not very delicately put. And it certainly wasn't a turn of phrase Reece could ever remember using before. But it so *perfectly* described how the Divine Diana had looked when she first opened the door and found him standing on the other side of it!

And she wasn't faring much better now either, burbling on about Puddle being the name of the cat that lay stretched out on one of the bean-bags. He didn't get the relevance of the introduction of the cat into the conversation at all. Unless she thought perhaps he didn't like them, or was allergic to them? As it happened he liked cats, approved of their detached independence from the people who thought they owned them; he respected their intelligence. He had never been able to appreciate hearing a woman being called a cat; he had never yet met any woman who portrayed anything like their majestic aloofness—not and actually meant it, that was!

And yet...

He studied Diana as she stood a short distance away from him. He knew a little more about her now, having called his assistant, Paul, once he had realised Diana had left Paris early this morning without seeing him, instructing the other man to have any information he could find concerning the model Divine available to him once he reached London. It hadn't even occurred to him that it wouldn't be; Paul was as efficient as he was highly paid, and only Reece knew he was the highest paid in the business.

Paul had two files waiting for him, one on the professional model Divine, the other one a personal file on Diana Lamb. Reece had been surprised at the briefness of the latter, barely three sheets of paper long, whereas the professional file was so thick with photographs and newspaper articles about her work that it had to be put on a desk to be read.

There had been hundreds—no, thousands—of photographs in this second file of the lovely Divine, of the model wearing everything and nothing—— No, never really nothing. The beautiful Divine had never been *that* sort of model, and, while Reece had been able to see the golden perfection of her body in minuscule swimwear, her nakedness had remained tantalisingly elusive. He had found those provocative photographs so much more erotic to look at than complete nudity could ever have been.

The personal file on Diana Lamb, for different reasons, had been just as frustrating. There was no childhood history at all, but, as this wasn't the part of Diana's life he was interested in, that hadn't disturbed him unduly. He might be able to find something in her background with which to hit Chris if the couple persisted with their relationship, but for the moment it wasn't too important.

The adult Diana Lamb, it appeared, led a very quiet life, no high-profile romances—he had asked Paul to check into there being any low-profile ones—no scandals either, just a calm, uncluttered life that didn't include family, and not too many friends either, friendship with this woman seeming to be an exclusive club not too many people were admitted to.

And yet Chris, his wayward, frivolously irresponsible son, had been allowed into that select club. That fact, for reasons he wasn't yet sure of, irritated the hell out of Reece.

And so the information Paul had managed to gather together about this woman, hastily as it had been done, didn't really tell him much more than he already knew: the model Divine was one of the highest paid in the business, while Diana Lamb was an extremely elusive woman.

'Puddle likes bread and cakes,' she impatiently explained her earlier warning about the cat now.

Reece turned to look down at the cat as it stretched before getting lazily to its feet. 'Stay!' he instructed softly, silver gaze meeting lime-green in a silent battle of wills.

The cat was the first to look away, falling back down on the big bean-bag before curling up and going back to sleep, looking for all the world as if he had never had any interest in the food so temptingly laid out before him.

Now if only he could elicit the cat owner's co-operation in the same way he might be in business!

As it was, Diana gave the sleeping cat a look that told it exactly what she thought of its disloyalty, before sitting down gingerly on the edge of the same big cushion.

Reece thought she looked even younger today without the heavy make-up she had been wearing the evening before for the show. In fact, she didn't look as if she was wearing any make-up at all today. And he could tell by the way the T-shirt reached baggily to her mid-thighs that she hadn't worn the body-hugging leggings for effect but for comfort.

If anything she looked even more beautiful today, that vulnerability he had sensed in her yesterday even more apparent, although, strangely enough, so was that inner strength he had been aware of too. She really was the most unusual woman he had ever met!

'Eat,' he instructed harshly, disturbed at the force of his growing attraction for the young woman he had only met at all because he wanted to evict her from his son's life. He certainly hadn't meant for her to take up residence in his own ordered life instead!

She met his gaze coldly. 'I'm not the cat!'

His mouth twisted derisively at the way it so obviously rankled with her that her cat had obeyed him instantly. It was just a rapport he seemed to have with felines, was certainly nothing personal. Although it relieved his own tension to know this woman hadn't liked it one little bit.

'You're far too skinny.' He was deliberately insulting, enjoying the responses he was getting from her now much more than the careful control he had encountered from her the night before. Obviously catching this young woman off-guard was the key to success where she was concerned.

She sat cross-legged on the cushion now, unselfconsciously alluring, a slight smile curving her lips as she shook her head. 'I'm an inch off being six feet tall, and an English size eight.'

He knew all that from her professional file, also that she had a body weight of only one hundred and thirty pounds, dark green eyes surrounded by sooty lashes, and waist-length hair that the Press seemed to describe as honey-coloured.

But away from the spotlights, her face youthfully free of make-up, the high prominence of her cheekbones seemed even more apparent, the line of her jaw sharper, the creamy length of her throat taking on a new fragility. And Reece was sure that, beneath the voluminous folds of that bright yellow T-shirt, the curves of her body would take on a more pronounced slenderness too.

For goodness' sake, he had come here to get her out of Chris's life, not concern himself with whether, because of her chosen career and the demands it made on her, she ate enough!

What was this man up to now? Why didn't he just get to the point of his visit and get it over with, because they both knew the only reason he was here talking to her at all was because of Chris. Or was this all part of his game-plan—lure her into a false sense of security, and then hit her straight between the eyes with his demand that she get out of Chris's life?

He sat back on his heels, eyes narrowed to steely slits. 'How much do you want to leave Chris alone?' he rasped harshly.

Ah. He was back on territory she understood now. But *he* didn't understand at all, because it wasn't 'how much' she wanted at all; it was something so much more than that.

Neither of them was at all interested in the array of food, and Puddle, opening one eye and seeing their indifference, decided it was all fair game, getting up slowly to pad over to the rug—and delicately help himself to a particularly succulent-looking pastry!

Because, like her, Diana was sure, the cat had known of Reece Falcon's lapse of control—an unfamiliar feeling for him. But she had guessed from the first that, where other things might fail to hit this man where it hurt, his son Christopher was definitely his Achilles' heel!

The silver gaze flickered only briefly over the disobedient cat as it slunk off into a corner to enjoy its loot, although Diana was sure the slight had clearly registered with this arrogant man.

'I said, how much?' he repeated coldly.

Diana eyed him pityingly. 'I've told you before, money doesn't interest me,' she said with obvious disgust for the crudity of the suggestion that it did. 'Perhaps it doesn't appear so to you, because I choose to live quietly, and because of the modest circumstances of this flat, but I'm a very wealthy woman in my own right because of my career.' Her years as a top model had been good ones, and she could now command thousands of pounds for just a day's work. She didn't need money from this man—she had enough to live in comfort for the rest of her life even if she should never work again. And at only twenty-one years of age, by anyone's standards, that was no mean achievement. Not that she was even considering retiring from the job she loved so much, but it was nevertheless, after years of hardship, gratifying to be secure in her own wealth.

'No one ever has enough money,' Reece Falcon rasped with contempt for the subject.

Only the very rich, who had never known any other way of life, could afford to be this arrogant. Reece Falcon had certainly never known what it was to want just enough money that you didn't have to be beholden to someone else for even the clothes you wore!

'I said I don't want your money, Mr Falcon,' she told him in a carefully controlled voice. She wouldn't touch his money. Not one single penny of the Falcon millions—tainted as it was with the blood and suffering of others. No, she didn't want any part of Reece Falcon's money.

His mouth thinned, dark brows raised in mocking scorn. 'Then what do you want, Diana? Chris?' he derided disbelievingly. 'A boy of twenty, who can't even begin to match your inner maturity?' He shook his head. 'I can't believe, knowing Chris as I do, that he can even begin to satisfy the needs of a woman like you.'

She knew he was being deliberately insulting, and yet she felt the colour drain from her cheeks anyway. 'Needs . . . ?' she repeated harshly. 'I don't——'

'Oh, but I'm sure you do, Diana.' Suddenly Reece Falcon was very close to her on the gaily coloured scatter-rug in front of the bean-bag she sat on. 'I think you know exactly what I mean by "needs".' He was so close now that his breath stirred the hair at her temple.

Every nerve in her body was screaming a protest, every brain cell she possessed recoiling in horror, as she knew, seconds before his mouth descended savagely on hers, that he was going to kiss her!

And it was like no other kiss she had ever known in her life before; it was totally demanding, erotically forceful, allowing no room for denial or rejection, just completely and utterly sensual, those warm lips moving over and against hers in a slow caress that seemed without end.

Try as she might—and she did try!—Diana's mouth couldn't escape his, and then, just when she thought she couldn't stand it any longer, she knew what she had to do, knew that she was approaching this all wrong; her response, *any* response, was what Reece Falcon wanted!

And so she went suddenly still, her arms falling to her sides, her body going limp in his arms, her mouth coldly slack and unmoving.

For long, timeless seconds, as Reece continued to kiss her, it seemed that wasn't going to work either. And then—miraculously to her, because she was starting to feel faint now!—he seemed to realise she was completely unresponsive, and his mouth stilled against hers even as he opened his eyes and looked down at her, her green gaze returning his with cold contempt for what he was doing to her.

He raised his head slowly, and Diana could see the flush slowly spreading under the tanned skin of his cheeks. Good; she hoped he burned with humiliation for what he had just tried to do!

He rolled away from her completely now, getting to his feet and running a hand through the dark thickness of his hair, his expression one of barely constrained frustration as he once again turned to look down at her.

Diana returned that look coldly as she too got slowly to her feet, relieved to find, as she did so, that the shaking of her legs wasn't visually apparent, even if she was fully aware of how unsteady they felt beneath her. Her hand moved up to push her hair back dismissively from her face, hair that seconds ago Reece Falcon had entangled his fingers in as he held her mouth against his. Oh, God, she mustn't think of that—couldn't, or she would go mad.

'*You* don't have the first idea how to "satisfy the needs" of a "woman like me"!' she told him with obvious contempt for his behaviour seconds ago.

A nerve pulsed in his tightly clenched jaw at the taunt. 'And you're telling me that Chris does?' he bit back glacially.

She met his gaze with contempt. 'I'm telling you nothing, Mr Falcon,' she scorned coldly. 'Because, you see, I don't have to——'

'I have the power to break you!' he told her with icy softness.

Diana didn't even flinch at the threat; he couldn't have used a worse word to her! 'I don't think so, Mr Falcon,' she returned with a calmness she knew was badly in danger of crumbling if she didn't end this meeting very soon. The power to break people; was that all this man understood? 'You see, Chris has asked me to marry him,' she told Reece Falcon triumphantly. 'And I'm still considering his offer.' Let him see how he liked someone else having the power for a change!

He looked as if he would have liked to physically hit out at her at that moment, although he visibly restrained himself, his hands clenching into fists at his sides. '"Consider" it all you want, Diana,' he bit out contemptuously. 'But I can assure you, you'll never be Chris's bride!'

She wanted at that moment more than anything to meet his challenge, to announce then and there that she *would* be marrying Chris, no matter what objections this man may make about it, so angry did she feel at his absolute certainty that she would never manage to marry *his* son. But to meet—and then feel she *had* to carry out—such a direct challenge didn't fall in with her own plans at all.

'Aren't you taking rather a lot for granted in assuming that I might want to be?' she scorned, her head back proudly.

'He's wealthy,' his father shrugged. 'Quite presentable——'

'But *your* son,' Diana put in softly. 'As you seem so fond of reminding me,' she derided.

Reece's mouth thinned. 'Chris won't be marrying anyone he knows I disapprove of,' he said with certainty.

The damned arrogance of this man! 'If I wanted to marry Chris,' she told him quietly, 'believe me, I would. With or without your approval!'

He looked at her with coldly glittering eyes. 'The day he married you I would throw him out of my organisation and disinherit him!'

She shrugged unconcernedly. 'Fortunately, I earn enough to keep us both.'

His eyes narrowed to steely slits now. 'Are you telling me that it wouldn't bother you having to work to keep your own husband?' He looked at her disbelievingly.

Diana shrugged again. 'Not in the least,' she dismissed with certainty; she had no intention of marrying Chris, but it wouldn't have bothered her if she had met and fallen in love with someone who had no money, if they should live mainly on her money. But the way this man thought he couldn't even begin to understand that sort of relationship, she realised contemptuously. 'If I cared about him enough,' she added tauntingly, 'it wouldn't matter which one of us earned the money.'

Reece's mouth twisted scornfully. 'And do you care about Chris enough to do that for him?' he challenged. 'Because if the two of you marry, it's a certainty that's what will happen.'

She gave a little half-smile, completely in control again herself in the face of his frustrated anger. 'I believe we were talking metaphorically, Mr Falcon, concerning the relationship I would have with my future husband. Whoever he might be,' she reminded him. 'As I've already told you concerning Chris's marriage proposal, I'm still thinking it over.'

'You——'

'But if I did decide to accept him, and you did carry out your threats——'

'Oh, I will,' Reece grated. 'Believe me.'

'Then you seem to have forgotten one important factor.' She shrugged unconcernedly. 'Chris *is* your son,' she reminded him hardly. 'And as such I can't see him being without some sort of career for long.' Chris might have been brought up as the son of wealthy parents, but as far as she could gather he had received no concessions from his father when he'd decided to enter his business, had had to prove himself first as an assistant to one of his father's assistants; in other words, he had been a general dogsbody for almost a year! No, she didn't doubt Chris would survive, no matter what his father decided about his future; Chris had the Falcon determination to succeed in life, although so far he didn't seem to want to do it by stepping on people the way his father had.

Reece Falcon looked at her with glittering eyes. 'I could ensure that neither of you ever worked again.'

She didn't doubt that he could carry out such a threat, but if he thought such a claim—truthful as it undoubtedly was—impressed or frightened her, he was mistaken. 'Then you're to be pitied rather than admired,' she told him with scorn. 'Because if you ever did such a thing, Chris would never forgive you.'

'Damn you!' Reece grated furiously at what he knew to be the truth, his jaw tightly clenched.

'Possibly,' she returned coolly. 'Now if you would excuse me...?' She arched mocking brows. 'Chris may be here in a minute, and I would like to look my best for him,' she added pointedly.

Reece Falcon looked as if *he* would dearly love to strangle her with his bare hands, controlling his rage with obvious effort, before turning on his heel and slamming out of the flat.

Only once Diana was completely sure he had gone, the door safely locked behind him, did she allow the trembling reaction to begin. And once it started she couldn't seem to stop it! She didn't know how often, or how successfully, she was going to be able to cope with meetings like that one.

But she had to. *Had* to!

Reece's anger lasted all the time it took his chauffeur to drive him across town to the penthouse apartment he had in London on the tenth floor of the prestigious building he owned.

But he knew, deep inside, that it was himself he was angry with above all else. Good God, he was jealous—*jealous*, damn it!—he who had never known the emotion before, with any woman.

Jealous of his own son's relationship with Diana Lamb...!

CHAPTER THREE

DIANA was still badly shaken when the doorbell rang a couple of minutes later for the second time that morning. If Reece Falcon had come back to issue more threats and dire warnings...!

But it wasn't him who stood on her doorstep this time when she wrenched the door open. 'Chris!' she greeted him weakly; she had mockingly made that challenge to Reece Falcon a few minutes ago about Chris's expected arrival here, but it hadn't been strictly true, and now that he was here——!

Good God, she was surprised the two men, father and son, hadn't actually met at the lift, one leaving, the other one anticipating seeing her again.

She wasn't quite sure in her own mind yet what she should say to Chris about his father; just that she had 'seen him' didn't even begin to cover those two momentous meetings she had had with Reece Falcon, but telling Chris the truth about them wasn't something she wanted to do either. Oh, she had no doubt that to do so would cause friction between father and son, but that wasn't actually what she wanted at this point in time. She would just have to stick to the 'seen him' explanation!

'You *could* look a little more pleased to see me,' Chris grinned teasingly, in complete contrast to his father in looks, his blond hair kept styled slightly overlong, warm eyes a deep shade of blue, his boyishly handsome face showing none of the cynicism his father displayed so readily.

Having actually come to like this impetuous young man, Diana deeply regretted that she might be the one to put the first lines of disillusionment on that charmingly attractive face.

But she couldn't develop a conscience over Chris; he was a Falcon, and all of that family had to be her enemy. All she had to do was keep remembering that all the time Reece Falcon had been destroying her father, her family, the secure life of nine-year-old Divinia, he had been lavishing love and money on his own child—Chris! All she had to do was make sure she never forgot that fact, reminding herself that perhaps it was time, in Chris's privileged life, that he did learn there were some people who could say no to him, that she intended doing so. But not yet. Not yet . . .

She returned his smile teasingly, moving to kiss him lightly on the lips, the two of them of a similar height, even with Diana standing in her bare feet; it was a source of deep irritation to him that if she did wear shoes with a heel on she instantly towered over him. She impatiently dismissed from her mind the recollection that Reece Falcon had been one of the few men she had met who would still be taller than her even if she chose to wear three-inch heels on her shoes!

'Of course I'm pleased to see you,' she told Chris lightly as she put her arm through the crook of his to pull him inside the flat and shut the door behind him.

'Then couldn't you show it a little more?' He gave a disgruntled grimace at the lack of passion in the kiss she had given him just now.

She laughed softly, back on familiar ground with this young man—not like with his father; that was like walking on an unmarked minefield. 'Not at eleven-thirty in the morning I couldn't, no,' she dismissed easily, balking slightly as they entered the comfort of her sitting-room and she saw the food Reece Falcon had put out on plates earlier and put on the floor. Although she recovered well—she thought. 'You see, I've been expecting you——' She indicated the plates of food; after all, she and Reece Falcon hadn't had chance to eat any of it, and Puddle had only sneaked off with one *little* pastry!

Chris's face lit up with pleasure at the sight of the food he thought she had got in for him, and Diana allowed herself to feel just a little guilty for not being instrumental in providing the food at all. But she didn't think, considering how unconstructive this morning's meeting between herself and Reece Falcon had been, that the older man was likely to mention to his son that he had brought the bread and pastries here with the intention of sharing them with Diana himself!

'My favourite!' Chris bit hungrily into an apple danish. 'And made as only the French can,' he added appreciatively after swallowing the last bite. 'How did you enjoy Paris?' he asked interestedly as she came back into the room with freshly poured coffee.

She grimaced, sitting down cross-legged on the floor beside him. 'About as much as I expect you liked New York!'

'Too much work and not enough fun,' he said knowingly. 'Although,' he added thoughtfully, 'I did manage to have dinner one evening with my mother while I was there.'

Cathy Reiter—she had remarried a fellow American a couple of years after divorcing Reece Falcon—had returned to her native country once the divorce became final and her ex-husband gained custody of their only child. Chris had always been sure his mother had made the move initially because his father made it so difficult for her to have any access to him. Over the next five years Chris had apparently seen very little of his mother, until, at the age of fourteen, he had braved telling his father that he would like to go to America to live with her for a while.

How galling that must have been for Reece Falcon, Diana acknowledged ruefully. When she had pressed Chris for his reasons for wanting to do that he had merely shrugged the subject off dismissively. But Diana would hazard a guess on its having something to do with the lack of any real foundation to his father's life and the fact that his mother had now remarried, was settled with her new husband, and was able, emotionally at least, to offer Chris more.

Reece Falcon had, predictably, objected to the mere suggestion of Chris's going to live with his mother, even for a short time. Whereupon Chris had shown himself to be as determined as he, and had run away from the school he boarded at. And been found and brought back by his father. And run away. And been found and brought back by his father. And run away *again*. By which time Reece Falcon had decided he had to admit defeat and allowed Chris, for two years only, to join his mother in New York. And those two years had renewed a bond between Chris and his mother that still existed today, no matter how long a time it was in between when they saw each other.

Diana felt her own curiosity about the woman who had been married to Reece Falcon for ten years. What sort of woman was she, not only to have held the dubious role of Reece Falcon's wife for that number of years, but also to have wanted to, knowing—and Cathy Falcon couldn't have helped but know after his own treatment of her!—how utterly ruthless he was?

She had come to the conclusion that Cathy Falcon was either as ruthlessly uncaring as her husband, or very stupid, to have built her own life, and that of her child, on the money and success that had been accumulated at the costly expense of others not quite so cleverly ruthless. There was a third alternative, of course, and that was that Cathy Falcon could actually have loved her husband so much that she hadn't *cared* how he made his money. But that third alternative was so unacceptable to Diana as to be totally unthinkable!

'How was she?' Diana asked lightly, drinking her coffee, but not touching the food; after all, Reece Falcon had bought it—no doubt with the wealth he had acquired from some other poor fool who had trusted him! The food would have choked her.

'Very well.' Chris nodded confidently, eating the pastries as if he hadn't seen food for a week—and maybe, after hours of aeroplane food, that was how he felt! He certainly didn't need to worry about putting on weight—he never sat still long enough to accumulate the pounds. 'My little sister seems to be bigger every time I see her,' he added ruefully, look-ing at Diana frowningly as she began to chuckle. 'What is it?'

'Your little sister *does* get bigger every time you see her, you idiot!' She smiled. 'Children have a way of doing that!'

'Very funny!' He grimaced at the teasing. 'You know very well what I mean.'

Yes, of course she did. When she had first learnt of Chris's five-year-old half-sister, who lived in New York with her mother, Diana couldn't help wonder-ing if it had been the unexpected arrival of this rival for his mother's affections that had triggered off his own desire almost six years ago to go and live with her in New York. But, even if it had been his initial rea-son for going, Diana had learnt over the weeks of knowing him that Chris was very fond of the little blonde-haired angel born into his mother's second marriage; that he carried the little girl's photograph around with him in his wallet, and produced it proudly if asked.

'I'm sure she was very pleased to see you too.' Diana squeezed Chris's arm with understanding for his af-fection for the little girl. She had often wondered if her own life might not have been different if Janette had been interested in having children of her own, in be-ing a proper stepmother to her too. But there would still have been Marco...

'Yes, she was.' Chris's hand covered hers to show he didn't mind the teasing—that, in fact, he rather liked it! 'Which brings us back to my original remark: how pleased are you to see me?' He looked at her a little anxiously.

She shrugged, doing her best to firmly push thoughts of Marco and those dark years from her mind. 'I told you——'

'Precisely nothing.' He sighed his disappointment. 'Which is what you—cleverly—do, most of the time.'

She frowned at how suddenly the conversation had become so serious. 'Chris——'

'Did you get the roses while you were in Paris?' he asked eagerly.

Because of the time-difference and their both having heavy workloads this last week, they hadn't had a chance to actually talk on the telephone. 'Yes, I did, thank you,' she smiled. 'But you really shouldn't have gone to all that trouble.'

'No trouble,' he dismissed easily, his expression suddenly intent. 'Did you get the message that went with them?'

She moistened lips that were invitingly pink, despite being bare of any lip-colouring. 'You were right about your father,' she nodded. 'He did come to——'

'I wasn't talking about that warning concerning my fath—— He did?' Chris's attention sharpened as he realised exactly what she had said. His thoughts had obviously been on that other message he had sent every day she had been in Paris.

Diana looked at him curiously; he seemed very agitated all of a sudden at the thought of his father having possibly been in Paris at the same time she was. Not that Reece Falcon didn't induce that sort of emotion in most people—including her?—but Chris was his son, after all.

ELUSIVE OBSESSION   67

'He did come to Paris, then?' Chris chewed on his bottom lip.

'Yesterday,' Diana nodded slowly.

Chris grimaced. 'Was he alone?'

Ah. Obviously Chris knew of the redhead's existence in his father's life. But did he also know of Reece Falcon's intention of making her his wife?

'Actually, no,' Diana answered lightly. 'He had a lady with him.'

'Hell,' Chris muttered aggressively. 'Did he—speak to you?' He looked anxious now.

'Briefly,' she dismissed truthfully, although if Chris knew his father at all he must know that Reece Falcon would only need to talk 'briefly' to someone to make his feelings perfectly clear!

Chris obviously did, and he swallowed hard. 'He wasn't—insulting, was he?' His gaze was searching on her face now.

Reece Falcon—insulting? Was the grass green? The sky blue? Blood red ...?

She shrugged dismissively. 'I told you, Chris, we only talked briefly, and that was in a room crowded with other people involved in the show.'

He looked uncomfortable now, standing up to pace the room, his hands thrust deep into the pockets of his suit trousers. 'That's good.' He nodded distractedly. 'You see, before I went to New York, he asked me about you, and I told him——' He broke off.

'Yes?' Diana prompted warily when he broke off so suddenly.

'I told him I was going to marry you!' he burst out defensively.

As well he might be—they both knew he hadn't even *asked* her at that time! But she admitted to herself she had known how he felt, had even known the proposal was imminent. Just as she had always known what her answer was—*had* to be when he did eventually ask her.

She met his gaze calmly. 'That was a little precipitate of you,' she said lightly. 'Even a little foolhardy. Didn't it even occur to you when you were making this claim that your father's curiosity might be a little piqued about this woman you claimed you were going to marry; that he might even come to Paris himself to take a look at me?'

All the tension suddenly went out of Chris, and he grinned at her affectionately. 'God, how I love this knack you have for understatement!' He began to chuckle. 'A little piqued,' he repeated, his eyes glowing merrily. 'My father's curiosity has never been "a little piqued" in his life!' He shook his head. 'He's been blazingly angry in the past, even glacially furious, but never *a little piqued*!'

It was a vaguely amusing term for her to have used to describe Reece Falcon now that she actually thought about it, but surely not enough to merit rolling around on the floor clutching his sides the way Chris was?

Although, on second thoughts, maybe it was, she decided as her own laughter bubbled up and threatened to be as uncontrolled as his was becoming.

She had to laugh at Reece Falcon or she would cry. And she had cried enough tears in her life because of that man already—she had no intention of crying any more. Not even tears of laughter.

Chris put his arms around her and hugged her. 'My father is going to love you as much as I do when he gets to know you,' he said with happy certainty.

Diana doubted that. She doubted it very much . . .

Reece glanced at the plain gold watch strapped to his wrist for what must have been the sixth time in as many minutes, irritated with himself intensely for the way he actually wanted to see Diana Lamb again; he certainly wasn't this uptight at the thought of having dinner with Chris—he had seen him at the office earlier, which was when Chris had issued the dinner invitation for Reece to join himself and Diana at the exclusive restaurant his son knew was one of his favourite places.

Were the young couple going to present him with a *fait accompli* when they *finally* got here, and announce their engagement? Had Diana Lamb stopped 'considering' Chris's offer, as she had claimed to be doing yesterday, and decided to accept him? Why else would Chris have arranged this dinner at all, knowing how Reece felt about the situation, if that weren't the case?

Reece couldn't help wondering how much his adamant declaration that Diana Lamb would never marry his son had actually influenced her decision to accept him. He couldn't have failed to notice how much his arrogance—and he accepted it as such!—in making such a claim had infuriated her. In that calmly controlled way that was such an integral part of her, that was.

God, it was that very control he sensed in her that so intrigued him! Even when he had kissed her—and he still gave an inward groan of self-disgust every time he remembered how he had been reduced to trying to *force* a response from her!—she had remained emotionally removed from him.

No other woman had ever intrigued him the way this one did, so much so that he had found himself thinking of her during the day when he least expected, or wanted, to do so; he *never* allowed thoughts of the women in his life to intrude when he was dealing with business issues. But Diana Lamb wasn't in *his* life; maybe that was the problem...

And then suddenly, without even having to look in the direction of the doorway, he knew Diana had arrived.

This restaurant, frequented by the rich and famous, and the rich who preferred to maintain their privacy, was never moved to curiosity about new arrivals. And yet at that moment all the conversation seemed to stop in the room, all heads turned expectantly towards the entrance.

Reece knew it *had* to be Diana, the beautiful Divine, who could capture the interest of such jaded diners.

He took a deep, steadying breath before raising his own gaze, that same breath becoming constricted in his throat when he saw her.

Good God...!

From the top of her glittering golden head, that gold sheen rippling down her back to the base of her spine, over the almost cosmetically free perfection of her face—she wore only a deep red lip-colour to emphasise the pouting allure of her full mouth—down over pertly uptilting breasts, slender waist, and gently curving thighs encased in a black sheath from neck to mid-thigh, a dress that clung so lovingly to every inch of her that nothing could be worn beneath, down the long golden length of her legs to the bare—yes, bare, Reece realised in amazement!—delicacy of her slender feet, Diana Lamb was every inch the beautiful model Divine!

His attention remained fixed on those bare feet; where the hell were her shoes, for God's sake? This restaurant might cater for the rich and famous—infamous, in some cases!—but even so, there was still a dress-code. Who did Diana think she was, coming here like that? It was going to put Brian, the owner, in a very awkward position if he had to ask her to leave.

And then, as she tucked her hand companionably into the crook of Chris's arm to walk over to the table where Reece was already seated, he realised she didn't have bare feet at all, that she actually wore a pair of completely flat see-through shoes. Not exactly Cinderella—the shoes weren't made of glass, and Diana wasn't a poor anything!—but there was no doubt that Diana Lamb was beautiful enough to attract the attention of any prince!

Much as Reece hated to admit it, she and Chris made a striking pair as they crossed the room, both being exactly the same height, both youthfully good to look at; they looked like a golden couple, with the whole world at their feet just waiting to be claimed.

But they weren't a 'couple'—never would be if Reece had his way—and the sooner the two of them were made aware of that, the better if would be for all of them!

He had come here alone to have dinner with them tonight for that reason only. He could have brought Barbara with him, but he had inwardly balked at the thought of the two women being together. He had known that, without wanting to, he would have made comparisons between the two—and that in every way Barbara would be the one found wanting! The type of fresh, untouched beauty that Diana possessed just wasn't fair to other women.

And so he had come here to the restaurant alone tonight, only to arrive on time himself and then be kept waiting twenty minutes for his son and Diana to arrive. And Chris was well aware of how he hated to waste time waiting for anyone!

He stood up now as the young couple reached the table, fixing his unrepentant son with a reproving glare. 'It's the height of bad manners to keep your own guest waiting at the table for you to arrive,' he rasped harshly.

'Oh, give us a break, Dad,' Chris grinned unabashedly. 'You're hardly a guest!'

His brows rose mockingly. 'Does that mean I'm the one picking up the bill at the end of the evening?'

Chris looked irritated now. 'Of course not,' he snapped. 'I don't know what all the fuss is about.' He shrugged dismissively. 'So we're fifteen minutes late——'

'Eighteen,' Reece heard himself correct, wondering why he didn't just drop the subject; it really wasn't that important. And yet—God, of all things, he couldn't help wondering what the hell these two had been doing during the eighteen minutes that had made them late!

He had no doubts whatever that if the two of them
wanted to make love they would do it at any time they
chose; in fact Chris could have spent the night with
Diana at her flat for all he knew, Chris having moved
into his own home over a year ago. And yet the
thought that that might have been what delayed their
arrival here tonight filled him with rage! It was unac-
countable, incredible—but true...!

Chris just looked more puzzled than ever by
the scene he was making over the whole thing.
'Look——'

'I'm afraid it's my fault we're late, Mr Falcon,'
Diana spoke for the first time that evening, her voice
low and husky. 'My hair took longer to dry than I had
anticipated.' She ran an apologetic hand through the
cascade of silken gold.

Reece watched the movement with what he knew
had to be hunger, wishing it could be his own hand
running through that golden length, a perfume as
elusive as Diana herself pervading his nostrils.

Any man, he knew, would forgive this woman for
keeping him waiting, if she looked as lovely as this
when she did eventually appear. Damn her!

'As I said,' he rasped hardly, 'it's the height of bad
manners to keep a guest waiting!'

Diana heard Chris's sharply indrawn breath at the
calculated insult. And coming from this man, knowing him as she did, she knew it was exactly that.

There was obviously—no matter what Chris might
have hoped to the contrary—going to be no quarter
given this evening by Reece Falcon towards the two of
them. He didn't approve of their relationship, Diana
inwardly acknowledged again as she sat down in the

chair Chris held out for her before sitting down in the chair next to her himself as his father finally resumed his own seat at the same time, and nothing was going to change his mind about that.

My God, she thought ruefully, it was just as well she didn't *want* it to!

She hadn't been quite clear what the next step should be concerning Reece Falcon, but when Chris had suggested this dinner together so that his father could 'see how wonderful she was' she had realised it was probably the next logical step. It would be what Reece Falcon would expect—and she had to give him a little of what he expected. Just a little. She was sure the answer to keeping his interest, with a man as jaded as he obviously was, was to constantly do the unexpected.

Chris was flushed with anger at the attack now. 'We have apologised, Dad——'

'It's all right, Chris.' She laid her hand deliberately over his as it rested on the table-top, knowing that glittering grey eyes were watching the movement—and disliking it intensely! 'Your father is quite right; it was naughty of us to be late when we were the ones who invited him out to dinner.' She looked across at Reece Falcon from beneath the dark sweep of her lashes. 'But I'm sure he'll forgive us...?' She smiled at him beguilingly, knowing that if he persisted in being such a bore after that charmingly made apology he was going to make a complete idiot of himself!

Obviously he thought so too, his mouth thinning with repressed anger at what he knew was her manipulation. Diana could appreciate how frustrating it must be for this, the king of manipulators, to be played at his own game—and lose!

'Of course,' he finally dismissed tightly. 'Perhaps you would like to order a drink, and then we can look at the menus?' he suggested pointedly as a waiter hovered near their table.

Chris was obviously still very disgruntled at his father's unreasonable attitude, although he relaxed slightly as they studied the menu together, their shoulders touching as they did so, their golden heads very close together.

The same couldn't be said of the man who sat opposite them! The longer she and Chris continued to linger over the menu, talking and laughing softly together as they did so, the more Reece Falcon's tension grew, his eyes an angry glitter of silver when Diana dared a brief glance at him from beneath lowered lashes, his mouth a thin slash of disapproval, deep lines grooved into his cheeks beside his nose and mouth, his jaw tightly set.

He was jealous of her closeness to Chris! Diana knew it as surely as if the words had been spoken out loud; knew it, and was inwardly triumphant at this crack in the rigidity of his self-control, a thrill of satisfaction coursing down her spine.

'If the two of you could stop making an exhibition of yourselves long enough for us to actually order some food...?' he finally rasped, no longer able to control the outburst, Diana realised with an inward smile.

But Chris was far from amused as, with a slam of repressed anger, he put the menu down, that they had been studying so light-heartedly seconds ago. 'Since

when has it been "making an exhibition" of yourself
to sit close to the woman you care about?' he challenged indignantly. 'Even in so public a place as a restaurant!' he neatly covered that argument, looking
challengingly at his father.

Since Reece Falcon had decided he didn't like seeing Chris sitting so close to her, Diana could have answered him! But she didn't. Let Reece Falcon get
himself out of this one alone. *He* was the one drawing
attention to himself, not them!

She gazed across the table at him with widely innocent eyes as she waited for his answer.

Cat. The little cat had claws, Reece realised as his
frustrated anger at seeing Chris with her began to fade
and be replaced by amusement. Those claws might be
kept sheathed most of the time behind that calm
aloofness she usually displayed, but underneath that
her emotions ran as deeply as everyone else's.

And at the moment she was enjoying his discom-
fort in having acted like a prize fool over her earlier
closeness to Christopher! She knew, this witch of a
child, that he wanted her for himself.

And God, how he wanted her. Exclusively. For as
long as it took him to satiate himself with that intriguing combination she had of cool calm and
youthful vulnerability. Because he *would* tire of it—he
had no doubt on that score—as he had tired of every
other woman in his life.

But until that time came he wanted her. In his arms.
In his bed. God, most of all he wanted that! Wanted
her silken limbs wrapped around his, that golden hair
entwined about his throat like a silken chain, those

green catlike eyes dark with a passion only he could assuage . . .

He could feel his body harden just at the thought of making love to this elusive Circe. Incredible. Absolutely incredible!

'I'm sorry, did you say something?' She arched dark brows in questioning innocence as he gave a low groan in his throat.

His mouth tightened at her barely concealed mockery. 'No,' he snapped tautly. 'Although, as Christopher well knows, I do have a lot to say concerning this relationship between the two of you——'

'Not now, Dad,' Chris put in hastily, shooting him a pleading look. 'Just get to know Divine——'

'Her name is Diana, as you very well know,' Reece rasped, still annoyed that he hadn't known that fact when he first met her.

Chris flushed at the rebuke. 'Well, just get to know her first, hmm?' he encouraged hopefully.

Get to know her? Good God, he wanted to strangle her for intriguing him the way she did when he barely knew her; wanted to take hold of the slender delicacy of her shoulders and shake her until—oh, God!—until he couldn't stop himself from kissing the provocative pout of her lips any longer!

'There would be little point in that,' he bit out tautly, furious at his own weakness in wanting this woman at all. He had known women more beautiful, damn it, sophisticated women who knew the rules of being a part of his life; he had a feeling Diana Lamb had her own set of rules for any man in *her* life, and that they were nothing like his! 'I doubt Miss Lamb

and I will meet often enough to warrant my ''getting
to know'' her,' he dismissed harshly, eyes narrowed.

Dark brows rose over deep green eyes. 'No?' Diana
challenged softly.

As if to prove her point, Chris's hand moved possessively over hers as it rested on the table-top, his expression one of ill-concealed fury as he glared across
the table at Reece. 'You may as well get used to the
idea, Dad,' he told Reece bitingly. 'Diana is in my life
to stay!'

Over his dead body!

Unfortunately, Reece had a strong feeling that, if
Chris did actually succeed in making this beautiful
young woman his wife, something inside Reece himself *would* shrivel up and die. The last thing he wanted
to be to Diana was her father-in-law! And as Chris's
wife she would be totally out of reach to him, forbidden fruit, no matter how the marriage should turn out.

He looked at Chris mockingly. 'Isn't that going to
be a little awkward?' he taunted pointedly.

Chris's frown became even fiercer. 'Don't do this to
me, Dad,' he warned softly.

His brows rose. 'Well—isn't it?' he drawled.

'I told you——'

'Don't tell *me*, Chris,' Reece bit out harshly. 'I'm
not the one you have to explain yourself to.'

'I——' Chris broke off resentfully as their first
course began to arrive. And by the time they had all
been served his angry retort to Reece's taunt no longer
seemed appropriate.

But those few minutes' respite hadn't frustrated
Reece in the way they had his son. On the contrary,
they had given him time to pause and reflect on Chris's

behaviour. There was something very wrong here. Chris was *too* defensive, almost as if—— But no, he must have *told* Diana; he couldn't have kept something that important to both of them to himself. And yet...when had it ever come up in conversation? Now that he had time to think about it, even when he had spoken to Diana alone yesterday, never once had either of them mentioned—— Damn it, he hadn't done so because he hadn't thought it necessary! But Diana didn't know, he was sure of it, and the more he thought about it, the more sure he became.

What the hell did Chris think he was playing at, keeping something like that from the woman he supposedly loved? Whatever it was, Reece knew he had him now. The only question now was, when did he reel in the stupid little fool and watch him flounder?

He could almost have felt sorry for Chris—if he didn't feel so damned relieved for himself that his son's romance with Diana Lamb would soon be at an end. It was a certainty that Chris wouldn't like it at all if Reece immediately tried to date Diana, but, knowing the relationship would be over, and soon, perhaps Reece could afford to be generous and wait a few weeks before making his own move. Diana might be a little more amenable too given a few weeks' uncertainty concerning his interest in her, which she so obviously knew about.

Yes, he had a feeling he was going to enjoy this meal after all. And then over coffee...!

Something in the balance of the evening had shifted tangibly. Diana could feel it in the changed atmosphere, in the way Reece Falcon was no longer the one who was tense and irritated but Chris now seemed to be, in the way the older man ate his food with gusto while Chris—and very soon Diana—merely pushed the food around the plate without really eating much of it.

It had something to do with that earlier conversation, when Chris had become so defensive. Although she couldn't for the life of her imagine what it could have been about. And Reece Falcon, from the smile of satisfaction on his lips, wasn't about to tell her until he was good and ready to do so! Like pawns on a chessboard, they waited for his next move.

And he was obviously in no hurry to make it. The three of them were at the coffee stage of their meal, Chris's tension almost at breaking-point as the meal painfully progressed, when Diana sensed another shift in mood; Reece Falcon was filled with an air of unhurried expectation now.

He turned to his son with dark brows raised in gentle mockery, and Diana instinctively reached out to clasp Chris's hand, for his sake not her own; there was nothing Reece Falcon could do or say now that would make the slightest difference to her own plans. But he couldn't know that; he was obviously enjoying the cat-and-mouse game he was having with Chris.

'I almost invited Barbara along tonight to make up a foursome,' he drawled softly.

That sounded harmless enough to her; it seemed only natural that he should want his fiancée in on a family problem. But Diana could feel Chris's tension at the statement, so perhaps he wasn't particularly fond of the woman his father intended marrying, and wouldn't welcome what he would see as interference in his life from her. Because Diana didn't doubt that the lovely Barbara would side with this autocratic man over Chris's interest in her.

All Diana really knew for certain about this was that she was being made a spectator to some sort of show Reece was setting up—a show in which he was undoubtedly the star *and* the director!

'But then I had second thoughts about it,' he continued with taunting mockery now, 'and realised just how inappropriate that would have been.'

Chris's face was very flushed, his expression pained. 'You——'

'After all,' his father added lightly, the look on his face deceptively innocent, 'one doesn't usually invite one's son's future mother-in-law along to meet his mistress!'

Chris indignantly denied this description of Diana's part in his life, but Diana barely heard him, her attention fixed frowningly on Reece Falcon as he sat across tne table from them looking so triumphant.

For a brief moment she had wondered, when he referred to the absent Barbara as Chris's future mother-in-law, whether he had made a mistake and actually meant to call her *stepmother*. But as she met the mocking challenge in Reece Falcon's glittering eyes she knew this man *never* made mistakes . . . !

CHAPTER FOUR

SHE hadn't known. Reece could clearly see that in Diana's slightly shocked expression as the full meaning of his words became apparent to her. But, to her credit, he acknowledged admiringly, it was an emotion she quickly masked as she sensed his interest in her reaction, and the smile she directed at him was one of cool dismissal.

Dismissal! God, this young woman was incredible. He had just, very effectively he had thought, 'put a spoke in her wheel', regarding her intentions towards Christopher, and she was calmly dismissing *him* as a result of it! His admiration—and desire, he admitted!—for her grew.

Chris's engagement—if indeed that was what it was—to someone else ultimately made no difference to her own plans. Once she had achieved what she set out to do, Chris could go back to his fiancée with her blessing. Indeed, she would dance at his wedding if her own plans worked out!

But just who was this fiancée? Diana had heard nothing of any permanent woman in his life either before or after she had met him, and surely if he was engaged to someone she would have raised objections—as Reece Falcon now was!—about the amount of time her fiancé was spending with the model Divine? But Chris hadn't mentioned having a fiancée either—although perhaps in the circumstances that might be understandable. Although how he had intended coping with two fiancées at the same time, if she had immediately accepted his proposal, Diana had no idea!

He glared across the table at his father now. 'That engagement was your idea——'

'You did your own proposing, Christopher!' Reece rasped harshly. 'No one twisted your arm.'

The younger man became flushed at what was obviously the truth. 'I knew it was what you wanted——'

'I don't recall that making a lot of difference in the past once you had decided on what *you* wanted,' his father said pointedly. 'And until a few short weeks ago——' he looked pointedly at Diana as he spoke '—Madeleine apparently suited you perfectly as a wife!'

Madeleine. So the fiancée had a name now. It was a pretty name too. Diana couldn't help but feel curious about whether or not the other woman matched her name. Probably, if Chris had wanted to marry her—he had a definite liking for beautiful women.

But still Diana had no idea why Reece should have even thought about bringing the girl's mother with him to dinner this evening. Unless—goodness, that was all a little neat!—Reece married the mother, and Chris married the daughter. It was the only explanation she could think of. And if that was the case then another question sprang to mind: why?

'Maybe because this time I was trying to please you,' Chris defended frustratedly. 'You had made it pretty obvious that a marriage between the two families would be a good business move. And you know I've always liked Maddy——'

'Obviously not enough to have spared her the humiliation of hearing of your relationship with Diana from another source,' his father accused disgustedly.

Chris gave a pained frown. 'Maddy knows?'

'Of course she knows!' Reece confirmed impatiently. 'God, give the girl credit for having some intelligence, will you?' he scorned. 'She's been back from Switzerland almost a month, and you've only found the time to see her half a dozen times since then. And as your photograph would invariably appear in the newspapers as Divine's companion for the evening I'm sure it soon became apparent what you were doing when you weren't seeing Maddy! Obviously the evenings when you *did* manage to see the girl you're engaged to were nights when Diana could spare you from her side.' He gave Diana a scathing glance. 'Or she had something better to do than cling on to your arm!'

'Or I was working,' Diana corrected calmly, not rising to his deliberate insult.

'Possibly,' he conceded with an abrupt inclination of his head, eyes glittering silver as his gaze raked over her mercilessly. 'Whatever the reason——' he turned back to his son—'*you* haven't exactly been the attentive fiancé to Madeleine since she came home from finishing-school.' His mouth twisted. 'I took both Barbara and Madeleine along to the Paris fashion show in an effort to atone for your tardiness.' And his derisive expression showed exactly how much he had hated having to do that!

Chris's cheeks were flushed. 'I could have——'

'Could have what?' his father cut in scathingly. 'Accompanied Madeleine yourself instead of going to the States?' he scorned. 'I'm sure she would have just loved sitting next to you while you sat and drooled all over Diana as she strutted up and down the catwalk!' He shook his head disgustedly. 'I never took you for a fool, Chris, but over this you've certainly acted like one!'

Diana felt almost sorry for Chris as he visibly cringed under this verbal condemnation—even if it was richly deserved! He *had* behaved like an idiot, continuing his engagement to Madeleine while being seen so publicly with her; he had to have known the other girl would see their photographs taken together and draw her own conclusions. As his father had!

Thank God she wasn't serious in her own interest in Chris. And she couldn't help but feel sorry for Madeleine, whoever she was. Chris was hardly behaving like the faithful fiancé, so it must be making the other girl wonder what sort of a husband he was going to make—if Madeleine still intended going through with the wedding at all...!

At the same time as she felt sorry for the other girl Diana also couldn't help wondering where Madeleine had been the night she modelled the wedding gown for Charles; she had hardly been the beautiful, but so obviously in her mid-thirties redhead who had been seated at Reece's side that night. Maybe the younger girl had decided not to come to the show that night once she realised Divine would be modelling. Although that didn't seem a very likely explanation; Diana knew that, in the same circumstances, she wouldn't have been able to curtail her curiosity about the woman her fiancé seemed to have become infatuated with.

'I want to marry Div—Diana,' Chris told his father stubbornly, turning to look at Diana now. 'I hadn't even seen Madeleine since Easter until she got back last month,' he defended almost pleadingly.

'Well, she certainly didn't forget about *you* the moment you were out of her sight,' his father put in impatiently. 'Probably the emerald and diamond engagement ring you gave her at Christmas helped to remind her!' he added drily.

Chris's face seemed to be permanently flushed at having been put on the hot spot in this way. He obviously wished at that moment that he had never heard of Madeleine or the engagement ring his father spoke of!

But Diana, at least, had the answer to one of the questions that had been bothering her: if Madeleine had been away in Switzerland most of the last year being 'finished', then it would explain why Diana had never heard of him being out with the other girl. Or the engagement.

Diana would probably have attended a similar school herself at that age if——

She turned sharply to Reece Falcon. 'Chris has done nothing wrong,' she told him icily. 'We've been out together a few times, something the media has chosen to pick up on, but there was certainly nothing in those occasions that his fiancée need concern herself with.'

'Diana——'

'Accept your let-out with good grace when it's presented to you, Chris,' his father advised harshly at his agonised protest, Reece's own gaze resting admir-

ingly on Diana as he spoke. 'And save everyone involved further embarrassment,' he added firmly as
Chris would have protested again, his silver gaze resting challengingly on his son now.

Diana had to secretly admire the neat way he had
turned the situation around to his advantage, so that
Chris had now been put in the position of not being
fair to her either if he continued to pressure for acceptance of their relationship. Admire it—but at the
same time despise it! Reece Falcon obviously had
some sort of business interest of his own tied up in
Chris's engagement to Madeleine; hence it was in his
interests to keep the engagement alive no matter what
the feelings of the other people involved. Diana was
sure, if there had been some advantage to Reece
Falcon by Chris being involved with her, he wouldn't
have objected to the relationship at all!

'Why don't you go and see Madeleine now? It isn't
too late,' his father suggested softly. 'Try and smooth
things over with her, offer abject apologies for being
a naughty boy,' he added with the ghost of a smile.
'Offer to take her shopping tomorrow if you have to;
we can spare you at the office.'

Diana's mouth twisted disgustedly at this insult to
the other girl's intelligence; she was offended on
Madeleine's behalf at having her bruised emotions
dismissed so callously. 'That's sure to placate her!' she
scorned, eyes flashing deeply green.

Reece looked at her mildly, his mouth twisted with
mockery as he easily guessed at her indignation. 'You
might be surprised,' he drawled confidently.

'Very!' she acknowledged sharply—although, remembering Janette's values in life, perhaps not . . .

Reece shrugged. 'You don't know Madeleine——'

'Neither do you if you seriously think my going over there now and offering to drag around the shops with her tomorrow is going to in any way appease her for the wrong she thinks I've done her!' Chris cut in disgustedly. 'Besides, I don't want to,' he added almost petulantly. 'Don't you understand, Dad? I don't want to marry Maddy any more; I want to break our engagement——'

'Then maybe you should be man enough to go to her and tell *her* that!' his father bit out with even control, his expression harsh, not a muscle or nerve twitching as he looked steadily at his son in silent challenge.

Chris returned that gaze uncertainly, moistening his lips nervously the longer it continued. 'And you?' he finally ventured. 'How would you feel about my doing that?'

Oh, Chris, Diana groaned with inward pity. Away from Reece Falcon he had proved himself to be entirely his own man, but obviously, when it came to opposing his father's will, he was no different from all the rest who were terrified of challenging him.

Except her. *She* would oppose this man to her last breath, to the very gates of hell themselves . . .!

Reece shrugged, totally relaxed and unconcerned as he sat back in his chair at the table. 'Why don't you try it and see?'

Chris's uncertainty deepened as he looked at his father searchingly, obviously unsure of his mood now.

Which was more than Diana was! She knew exactly what Reece Falcon's emotion would be if Chris dared to break his advantageous—to Reece!—engagement to Madeleine. And it certainly wouldn't be approval for at least having done the honourable thing!

Finally Chris's gaze wavered and then dropped away completely as he too seemed to realise that; he sighed raggedly. 'I had hoped that meeting Diana might make a difference to how you felt about things, might make you realise——'

'Might help compromise me into feeling differently, you mean,' his father accused knowingly.

'*No!*' Chris protested frustratedly. 'I thought once you had realised what a wonderful lady she is, how beautiful——'

'Oh, I've realised those things,' Reece put in softly, looking at Diana with narrowed eyes.

Chris's expression brightened. 'Then——'

'—and they make absolutely no difference to her unsuitability in your life,' Reece continued as if he hadn't interrupted.

But a marked one to her suitability in *his* life, Diana realised slowly: Reece Falcon wanted her himself!

If Chris didn't leave soon Reece knew he was going to snap completely and actually order him out of here!

He just wanted to be alone with Diana Lamb now. His senses were attuned to her every movement, every graceful gesture of her hands—hands that he wanted against his body, caressing him. And her perfume was driving him wild, that tantalising, elusive perfume that totally suited the beautifully elusive woman she was— God, it *was* her; Charles Oxley had marketed a perfume earlier in the year that he had called Divine. And

Reece knew that Diana had to be wearing it at this moment. It was driving him slowly out of his mind!

'I'll take Diana home while you get a taxi to Madeleine's,' he announced arrogantly, signalling for the bill to be brought to him instead of the coffee the waiter had come over to offer; Reece knew he had to get out of here now, and with Diana at his side.

Chris looked stunned by his suggestion, and Diana—Diana just looked at him with that calmness of hers, revealing none of her inner emotions.

God, how he would like to see this woman burn with desire, all cool veneer gone as her passion matched his own! That moment couldn't come soon enough for him!

'I think the sooner you heal the rift between yourself and Madeleine, Chris, the better,' he told his son decisively, his tone brooking no argument to the arrangements he had suggested for their departure.

And he wasn't being completely selfish in this— quite a lot, but not completely! He actually had no doubts that Chris would eventually marry Madeleine, if not now, then some time in the future. The couple had known each other for years, were ideally suited, understood each other. It was just as well Madeleine understood Chris at the moment, otherwise he would be in more trouble than he actually was!

One thing Reece was absolutely certain of was that Chris was not going to marry Diana Lamb! If what Diana had said about their relationship was to be believed—and he had no doubt that this woman would rather use honesty to wound than lies!—then she and Chris had never been lovers. And now Reece knew they never would be.

Chris still looked rebellious. 'I told you, I don't want I can pay my own way, thank you!' He snatched the bill from in front of Reece as he would have been the one to pick it up.

Reece raised dark brows. 'Can you?' he queried softly. Pointedly. He hated doing it, but it was time Chris realised, once and for all time, that he held the purse strings—— God, he groaned inwardly with self-disgust, what the hell was he doing? Did he really want Diana Lamb so much himself that he was willing to threaten his own son to get her? The answer—painful as it was to admit it—was yes!

Thankfully Chris was too agitated himself by this time to take exception to the veiled threat, his movements aggressive as he dealt with the bill.

Reece almost felt sorry for him. If it had been any other woman but Diana——!

But it wasn't, and Reece wanted her for himself, could feel his tension rise as Diana sat forward to touch Chris's arm as she spoke to him so softly that Reece couldn't hear what was being said—even though he did try!

So instead he could only look at her, at the way her curtain of hair had fallen forward, so thick and luxuriant that Reece just wanted to entangle his hands in it—at the same time his body became entangled with hers! He felt like a callow youth as he felt his body harden with desire, knowing that he couldn't get up and leave the table just yet without totally betraying himself.

His attention tensed as Diana finally stopped talking to Chris in that undertone and looked across at Reece with those unfathomable green eyes. So cool, so calm, and yet she commanded interest—his, at least!—without even trying!

'As Chris and I came together by taxi,' she spoke softly, 'we appreciate your offer to drive us both home.' There was challenge in her voice now.

Because they all knew it wasn't what he had offered at all. But he could see it was a way of saving face for all of them. And that Diana had achieved it with the minimum of fuss...

It would also mean, once he had Diana safely inside his car, that his plans for being the one to take her home weren't completely lost. Although he didn't for a moment fool himself into thinking she had engineered it that way! Why was it that this particular young lady, the one he was finding he wanted badly enough to even cut out his own son, didn't seem in the least impressed by him, and made no effort to hide the fact? Oh, he had never fooled himself into believing it was the way he looked that brought most women he desired into his life, usually for as long as he wanted them there. He had learnt long ago that money and power were compelling aphrodisiacs for a lot of women. And he had plenty of both.

He wasn't always successful in winning the women he wanted, even with those powerful weapons at his disposal, but any rebuff usually meant there was already someone in those women's lives whom they loved and wanted to be with, and Reece could only respect them for feeling that way.

Diana Lamb didn't even pretend that her own lack of interest in him was because of any of those reasons—she had just scorned him from the beginning!

He didn't believe either that it was because this particular woman had enough money of her own not to be attracted to Reece's millions; there was a saying that 'you could never have too much money', and Reece happened to believe that was true, believed that money begat more money. Unless you were a fool, and lost it all on a game of chance. But that would involve taking a risk, and Reece only ever gambled on certainties.

However, he was far from certain about Diana Lamb...

Reece was so obvious in his intention of dropping Chris off at his apartment first and then driving her home that Diana was surprised at his lack of finesse in trying to achieve it. Or maybe he was just so determined to have his own way that he didn't care how he did it. Whatever, he had seated her beside him in the front of the black BMW, and a disgruntled Chris sat in the back glowering at them both, already excluded by the mere fact of the seating arrangement.

Diana could see that this was turning into a battle of wills between herself and Reece, and if he thought he was going to win as easily as this he was going to be sadly disappointed. And soon!

There was a look of triumph on the strong angles of his face once he had parked his car outside Chris's apartment building, although it was masked slightly as he turned to look at his son. 'I'll call you tomorrow, Chris,' he said lightly. 'I'll just drive Diana home now.'

He really did think it was as easy as that, Diana realised with an incredulous shake of her head. 'It's

very kind of you,' she drawled dismissively, releasing
the catch to her seatbelt as she spoke, 'but, as I'm sure
you can appreciate...' she gave him a bright, daz-
zling—and totally meaningless!—smile, as she knew
he had sensed the brush-off he was about to receive
'...Chris and I really do have a lot to talk about still.'
She opened her car door and got out, pointedly waiting on the pavement for Chris to join her.

A heavy scowl had settled on Reece's arrogant features. 'I thought I was taking you home,' he bit out
tautly.

'You have,' she nodded. 'It was—interesting,
meeting you again,' she added dismissively, green eyes
meeting the fierceness of his silver gaze in mocking
challenge.

'Oh, I have no doubt,' he ground out forcefully,
putting the car into gear with barely controlled movements once Chris had got out of the car on to the
pavement beside her, 'no doubt at all that we shall
meet again!'

She arched dark brows. 'Really?' she returned
softly. 'I can't imagine in what circumstances.'

His mouth thinned. 'And it will be sooner than you
think!' he assured her harshly, turning coldly to look
at his son. 'Tomorrow,' he told Chris again in a
warning tone before pressing the button to close the
window and driving off at great speed.

If Diana was relieved to have a respite from the open
as well as subtle undercurrent of Reece Falcon's challenging presence, it was mild in comparison to how
Chris obviously felt!

'God!' He physically wilted after the onslaught. 'That was so much worse than I ever imagined it was going to be!'

Her mouth twisted wryly at his naïveté. 'What did you think your father was going to do, Chris—pat you affectionately on the head and tell you it's perfectly acceptable to ask one woman to marry you while still engaged to another one?' Diana shook her head derisively. 'He's naturally furious with you,' she ruefully pointed out the obvious.

And in the circumstances—Reece Falcon's own relationship with Madeleine's mother—that wasn't in the least surprising! Chris's behaviour with her could obviously seriously damage that relationship too. Not that Diana cared about that, but it was clear Reece Falcon did!

'And you?' Chris looked at her almost pleadingly. 'Are you furious with me too?'

She didn't care about him enough in that way to be furious with him, but if she had actually intended marrying him then she would have been feeling quite differently from the way she did at this moment about his behaviour. 'I think——' she chose her words carefully '—that you've been very silly. I don't know how you even thought you could get away with your father and me meeting in that way and he—at least—not mentioning that you already have a fiancée.' She shook her head disbelievingly.

'I honestly didn't think he would do that to me,' Chris groaned painfully. 'I thought that by bringing the two of you together tonight in the way that I did I could force his hand in accepting our relationship.'

Diana could see that he really had believed that by presenting his father with a *fait accompli* he would be able to simply change fiancées with the minimum of fuss. How incredibly naïve this boy was! Reece Falcon was the manipulator, not the one to be forced into doing something he didn't want to do. Ever.

'It didn't work out that way, did it?' she mocked lightly.

'No.' He sighed heavily. 'And did you mean what you said to him earlier—that our going out together had been just that to you; that you have no intention of marrying me?' He looked at her with pained blue eyes.

She gave a rueful shake of her head at his hurt-little-boy look. 'Chris, you had no right even mentioning marriage to me,' she reminded him exasperatedly.

'You mean because of Maddy——'

'Of course I mean because of Maddy!' she confirmed impatiently. 'Look, we had some good times together, I've enjoyed your company, but now I think it's time you accepted that you already have a fiancée, and that I——'

'Yes?' Chris cut in sharply, frowning. 'Did you meet someone else while you were in Paris; is that it?' he accused.

She didn't believe this! 'Chris——'

'Because you haven't been the same since you got back from there; you seem more distant, less—affectionate.'

Considering the most they had ever shared had been a few kisses—carefully controlled ones on her part at that—this last accusation was verging on the ridiculous! Chris was trying to make them sound like lovers, with the love having cooled on her part.

'There's no one else, Chris,' she told him softly, knowing there possibly never would be anyone for her. Her obsession over Reece Falcon was such a dominating part of her life now, and it wouldn't be fair to offer any man less from a relationship than he deserved. Reece Falcon had done that to her... 'But at the same time I never had any intention of marrying you, Chris,' she added coldly. 'I wouldn't have gone out with you at all if I had realised you had a fiancée.'

She wasn't absolutely sure this latter claim was true, because she knew she had needed Chris to make the initial contact with Reece Falcon. But Chris had known full well of his fiancée, and he didn't particularly deserve her consideration now. He had proved himself to be his father's son—utterly selfish when it came to something he wanted. It was Madeleine she felt sorry for now, and she wondered if the other girl really did deserve Chris in her life.

'Why, you——!' Chris recoiled as if she had struck him. 'You knew how I felt about you, led me to believe——'

'Nothing,' Diana put in flatly, looking at him with hard green eyes. 'Absolutely nothing. I haven't deceived you in any way, Chris.' She shook her head. 'I never told you I loved you, never gave you any false hopes. It was your king-sized Falcon ego that did that!' she couldn't stop herself from adding hardly.

'Falcon ego...?' Chris echoed slowly, more than a little dazed by this unexpected attack from her when she so rarely deviated from that serenely calm exterior she usually presented to the world.

In fact Diana was disappointed in herself for the lapse; she couldn't start to become over-emotional now, when she still had a very long way to go.

She gave the ghost of a smile. 'After meeting your father, it's obvious where you get your determination from.' But in the father it was arrogance, pure and simple! 'We've had fun, Chris,' she shrugged, her smile warming slightly. 'Let's part as friends, hmm?' she encouraged.

His uncertainty dissolved to be replaced almost by panic as he realised, once and for all, that Diana was actually saying goodbye to him, and his hands reached out instinctively to clasp both of hers, his expression beseeching. 'But it's you I care about——'

'Sure?' Diana teased; if he wasn't still in love with Madeleine then why hadn't he made more of an effort to break the engagement? It could just be—in fact it probably was—that with the other girl's prolonged absence in Switzerland Chris had just forgotten how much he did care for Madeleine: absence didn't always make the heart grow fonder!

He looked shamefaced now. 'I'm so confused—it isn't funny, damn it!' he scowled as Diana began to chuckle wryly.

She shook her head, sobering slightly, although a smile still curved the natural pout of her lips. 'I'm not laughing at you, Chris, only at the ridiculousness of the situation. Usually it's the woman who's "so confused"!'

For a moment he remained unyielding, and then he gave a rueful smile of acknowledgement. 'I suppose it is pretty silly,' he finally conceded. 'But—well, the truth is, I don't want to lose you, Divine.'

'There's another way of looking at it, Chris,' she shrugged. 'You never really had me.'

Blue eyes widened at the starkness of the statement, and then he frowned. 'No,' he said slowly. 'No, I never really did, did I?' he realised regretfully.

Diana moved to kiss him lightly on the cheek; after all, her war was with his father, not with him. 'Take your father's advice and go and see Madeleine, if not tonight, some time soon,' she told him softly. 'Even if it's only to say goodbye.'

'Hmm,' he sighed heavily. 'I owe her that, don't I?'

'At least,' Diana nodded.

'And if I do say goodbye can I come and see you? No,' he dully answered his own question at her ruefully mocking expression.

'It's over between us, Chris,' Diana confirmed almost gently.

He scowled. 'And once again my father has his own way! You can't imagine just how galling that is.' He shook his head frustratedly.

Oh, yes, she could, only too well! 'I won't tell him if you don't.' She couldn't quite manage to keep all of the pent-up bitterness out of her voice, but luckily Chris was just so relieved to hear her say that that he was too self-absorbed to notice her vehemence.

'Let him stew for a while,' he agreed with satisfaction, obviously brightening at the prospect of bettering his father for a while, at the same time acknowledging his relationship with Diana was over mainly because of his own stupidity in deceiving her in the way he had and believing he could get away with it.

Diana's own smile lacked humour. It suited her own purposes not to let Reece Falcon know—yet—that his son no longer played a part in her life. 'I hope things work out for the best with Madeleine, whichever way that might be,' she said with quiet sincerity, aware once more that she had genuinely come to like Chris.

He looked at her with regret. 'You won't change your mind...?' he said hopefully as he sensed she was weakening. 'No,' he accepted again dully as she made no reply to what they both knew was a silly question. 'God, what a prize fool I've been!' he groaned self-disgustedly.

Diana chuckled softly with understanding for his inner frustration with himself. 'It's a fallacy of every human being, Chris,' she comforted.

He scowled again. 'Not my father.'

She sobered instantly. Oh, yes, Reece Falcon had been a fool at least once in his life that she knew of—twelve years ago when he had pushed her father to the extreme of taking his own life. And, like all fools, Reece would have to pay the price in the end.

And what a price he would pay.

Her hair rippled with vitality as she walked; it looked like silver in the moonlight rather than the gold it really was.

Reece sat in the shadowed interior of his car, parked across the street from Diana's flat.

He had been sitting here for two hours now. Waiting. Waiting for her to come home. Waiting to see if she would come home at all or if she would spend the night with Chris. With his son.

And as he had waited, the minutes slowly ticking by, he had raged—and suffered!—at the thought of Diana in Chris's arms, in his bed, that silken body entwined with his son's. He had ached until it had become an actual physical pain in the very pit of his stomach.

And yet now here she was, almost ethereal in the moonlight, tall and slender, silver and black, her feet still giving the appearance of being bare in those ridiculous see-through shoes.

But it was almost two hours since he had left her with Chris outside his son's flat. What had happened between the young couple in that intervening time? Had they made love, as he had imagined they had, only for Diana to leave afterwards? Reece knew that if he made love to Diana he wouldn't *let* her leave afterwards, that he would want her there with him all night, to love again in the morning. But Chris wasn't him, and—oh, God!—he was starting to hate his own son for the relationship he might have with this elusive—only to him?—woman!

Diana, head high, her step light, was totally aware of the car parked opposite as she took out her key to let herself into the building; of the car owner sitting silently behind the wheel in the shadows. Of Reece's burning, ever-growing anger. At her. At Chris. At himself.

It had begun.

CHAPTER FIVE

NEW YORK, a city that never seemed to sleep, seemed to Reece, after only one day among its bustling activity, to be boring and colourless.

He had flown to the States the day after that dinner with Chris and Diana, ostensibly because he genuinely had business to deal with there, but really because he wanted to talk to Cathy about the wedding; he owed her that much consideration, at least.

Over lunch his ex-wife, Chris's mother, had been warm and friendly, as beautiful as ever, their conversation containing none of the antagonism that had coloured so much of the last years of their marriage. In fact, it had all been so pleasant, it might almost have been cosy!

Cathy watched him with smiling puzzlement as they lingered over coffee at the end of the meal. 'What is it, Reece?' she prompted softly.

He looked up from his coffee-cup, frowning. 'Sorry?'

Her mouth quirked. 'You take your coffee black, with no sugar, and yet for some reason you've been stirring the bottom out of your cup for the last five minutes!' she said pointedly.

He looked down at the submerged spoon, dropping it down into the saucer as he realised she was right. He hadn't even realised he was doing it!

Cathy tilted her head questioningly; at thirty-eight she was still youthfully lovely to look at, the happiness she had found from her second marriage and family obvious from the glow to her dark blue eyes and the soft curve to her lips. 'And you haven't glanced at your watch once in the last hour,' she added with amusement.

It had been a past criticism of hers that he lived his life by the clock, that she even suspected he had it written down in his diary somewhere the nights he had to spend at home with her: 'Seven p.m. until seven a.m.: spend with Cathy!'

It hadn't been true, of course, but he had to admit that over the years he had learnt that time was a precious commodity, and that, if he didn't run his private as well as his business life on a tight schedule, sooner or later one of them suffered as a consequence. Obviously Cathy had thought one of them had anyway!

He returned her smile now self-derisively. 'I've been so enchanted by your company that time has become irrelevant,' he returned with mocking humour, enjoying this new lighter side to his relationship with Cathy; it seemed that now, finally, after years of marital disharmony, and the bitterness since, they could laugh together about the things that had so rankled all those years ago.

Cathy gave a splutter of laughter, causing several male heads in the restaurant to turn and look at her admiringly, a fact she was totally unconcerned with.

Reece knew that, for all the problems they had had in their marriage, Cathy had always been completely faithful to him, as she would be to Lewis now.

'You've never been so "enchanted" by any woman's company that "time became irrelevant" to you!' she scorned now.

She was wrong, he realised frustratedly. Diana Lamb—Divine—was never far from his thoughts. In fact, he didn't think she had been out of them since the moment he met her! Oh, he was carrying on with the running of his life in the way that he normally would, functioning automatically on the business side of things, his private life non-existent at the moment— because inwardly he felt the way a dog must do as it went round and round in circles apparently chasing its own tail! Damn the woman!

Cathy was watching the myriad emotions flickering across the usual withdrawn hardness of his face. 'Or have you . . .?' she said slowly.

He straightened in his seat, determinedly putting Diana from his mind; he *had* to stop thinking about her! 'No,' he acknowledged ruefully, knowing that he mustn't once let Cathy guess at his inner turmoil; one of her faults, he had found in the past, was a determination not to let go of things once she got on to them. 'You haven't told me how your lovely daughter is yet?' he prompted with a lightness he was far from feeling.

The frown didn't leave Cathy's brow as she wasn't fooled for a minute. 'Reece——'

'Leave it, Cathy,' he rasped, his hand resting briefly on hers on the table-top to take the sting out of his words. 'Chris tells me that Kelly should be starting

school next summer?' he encouraged, and thankfully
this time Cathy finally took her lead from him and
began to talk about her daughter, a subject very dear
to her heart.

Reece only half listened. He *would* forget Diana
Lamb. She wasn't for him. Couldn't be for him.

But *God*, how he wanted her!

Reece was back in her life. It had taken almost four
weeks, four tension-filled weeks when Diana had
thought she must have misread the situation, and then
today, on returning from a modelling assignment being photographed in Antigua, her agent had telephoned her to say Carlton Cosmetics had called and
had an interesting proposition to put to her.

Reece Falcon *was* Carlton Cosmetics.

Diana knew every business he owned or even partly
owned, as he did this cosmetic company, knew everything he owned, had made it her business to know.
And the offer from Carlton Cosmetics for her to do
some work for them was too much of a coincidence in
those circumstances; even though the offer had come
from one of the senior executives, and seemed to have
nothing to do with Reece Falcon, she didn't doubt for
a moment that he was behind the offer.

She had turned it down without asking for any details. Flatly. Unequivocally.

Her agent was stunned by her reaction, and seriously advised her against doing any such thing. This
was the sort of contract most top models longed for—
to be taken on exclusively, by a cosmetic company especially, to promote their lines. It usually meant the
models concerned had reached the top of their pro-

fession if companies were willing to offer them hundreds of thousands of pounds just for their face and figure, and the monetary aspect of this offer was absolutely enormous; no wonder Bea had been so upset by her refusal. But Diana had seen it for exactly what it was—a tempting carrot being dangled in front of her nose. And so she had remained adamant despite Bea's persuasions, finally reminding Bea of her other commitments for the next year. Bea had instantly come back with the fact that Carlton Cosmetics appreciated that, and were willing to fit their own schedule of work for her around those commitments.

It was so very obliging of them—and to Diana it just smacked of Reece Falcon being determined to have his own way. And what he wanted was to have her under contract to work for his company—although that really meant him!—and so in his mind put her under a certain obligation and subservience to him too!

She felt absolutely no qualms about turning down the offer, although the fact that she had been approached at all by the company filled her with a certain elation. Reece Falcon obviously hadn't been able to forget her as easily as he had thought he would when he had made what she was sure was a conscious decision not to see her again, which, after all this time had elapsed, she had thought—feared!—he might have done.

But she was sure now that all she had to do was sit back and wait for the next development. Because she didn't doubt—not now—that there would be one.

It had been a long four weeks, a time when she had kept an avid eye out for an announcement in the newspapers of Reece's forthcoming marriage to

Barbara, sure as the days slowly passed and she heard nothing from him herself that the announcement had to be imminent. But there had been nothing at all about such a marriage. Diana could only assume that the other woman had come to her senses and changed her mind, or else it was Reece who was dithering at the commitment. All that really mattered—to Diana, at least, was that there had been no announcement.

'What do you say, Puddle?' she chatted as she absently fed the cat after talking to Bea on the telephone. 'The fish is certainly biting, hmm?' she said with satisfaction, easily able to envisage Reece Falcon's frustrated anger when told of her reply to the offer.

'Go back and offer her more money,' Reece told his assistant grimly.

'I've already suggested that,' the efficient Paul told him with a shrug. 'Explained that part of the contract is negotiable, within reason.' He made a face. 'Her agent seemed to think it wouldn't make any difference. Look, Reece, I don't know a lot about the modelling world, but it seems to me that what this model Divine has been offered is already far above——'

'You're right, Paul,' Reece cut in coldly, 'you know nothing about it!'

Damn her, how dared she so arbitrarily turn down this offer Carlton Cosmetics had made to her? She hadn't even asked for time to think it over; her answer had been almost immediate. And, as Paul had already pointed out, the monetary side of the offer was more than generous, with the other conditions of the

contract all in her favour too—a fact his legal depart-
ment had pointed out with some trepidation.

He had spent the last four weeks forcing himself to
stay away from her. From New York he had gone to
Las Vegas, but instead of winning on the roulette table as he usually did—the only form of gambling he
ever indulged in—he had lost heavily.

And it had been the same with everything he did in
the weeks that followed, business deals turning sour as
he felt none of the usual excitement of the challenge
coursing through his veins. And as for his personal
life——! Beautiful women: young, experienced,
blonde, redhead, brunette—all had passed through his
life during the mad social whirl he had made of his
leisure time the last four weeks—and he hadn't wanted
one of them, hadn't even felt a flicker of desire towards any of them!

Green catlike eyes haunted him, awake or in his
dreams, and he only had to close his eyes to feel the
length of her body pressed against his. Once. He had
kissed and held her *once*, damn it—and he hadn't
stopped wanting her since.

One thing seemed to have gone right the last four
weeks, at least—Chris's patching up his relationship
with Madeleine. And yet, frustratingly for Reece, at
the same time his son refused to confirm or deny that
his relationship with Diana was over. There had been
no further photographs of the two together in the
newspapers, but, considering the shaky state of Chris's
relationship with Madeleine, this wasn't so surprising; if Chris was still seeing Diana, he would obviously do it in private from now on. Reece just wanted
to strangle him for being so bloody-minded and not

saying outright one way or the other, but, as this stubborn unwillingness to conform was a characteristic Chris had got from him, there wasn't much he could do about it!

And the real truth of the matter was that Reece felt as if he was losing control of all aspects of his life. And he knew it was his obsession with Diana that was causing it. In the end, the only way of dealing with it seemed to be to see Diana again, to rid himself of his need for her once and for all.

It had seemed like a gift from the gods when he'd learnt of Carlton Cosmetics' need for a famous face to show off their new line of make-up due to be launched in the next few months—he'd immediately thought of Diana. She was beautiful, a face of the moment, and it had only taken a few minutes to check that, apart from her exclusive work with Charles Oxley, she wasn't under contract to anyone else for promotion work on this scale. Best of all, it was a way for Reece to see her again without sacrificing his pride into the bargain! There hadn't been a single voice of dissent when he had suggested the beautiful model Divine for their advertising.

Except from Diana herself...!

Reece had been furious when Paul came and told him she had refused the offer, and he knew from his assistant's puzzled looks that he was surprised at the vehemence of his boss's feelings over what was supposedly just another business contract. But the truth of the matter was that Reece felt at a complete loss to know what to do next. Impotent. And it wasn't a feeling he liked at all.

Suddenly he came to a decision, standing up abruptly. 'I'll deal with this matter myself from now on, Paul,' he rasped grimly. 'No reflection on your capabilities,' he added to soften the blow when he could see the other man had taken this decision as a critical reflection on his own lack of success. 'I just happen to know the lady,' he said ruefully, knowing he could have added that he also knew how bloody-minded and unreasonable Diana Lamb could be, that he could even sympathise with Paul's amazement that the offer of more money hadn't made the slightest impact on Diana.

It seemed that Diana had meant it when she'd said she couldn't be bought. At least, not with money, anyway. But there had to be something she wanted . . .

One of the things that Reece wanted to know was did she actually know he was behind the Carlton Cosmetics offer, or had she just turned it down at random? Was the rebuff a deliberately personal one to him, or was it unknowing . . . ?

A meeting, Bea had said persuasively. Just a meeting with the top executives of Carlton Cosmetics. Talking to them couldn't do any harm at all, her agent had cajoled as Diana still didn't look impressed.

Because she had known it wouldn't do any good either! There was no way Diana would ever be persuaded into working for Reece Falcon, or any company he was involved with, in any capacity, under any conditions—generous as the ones Carlton Cosmetics were offering her were! She dealt with Reece Falcon on her own terms only.

Nevertheless, she had finally agreed to go along to the meeting at the Carlton Cosmetics office in London, refusing Bea's offer to come with her, preferring always to deal with things like this herself. A lot of the top models dealt with the business side of their career nowadays—it was one of the things that made them so different from the models of the eighties. Besides, she knew there was no reason for Bea to drag herself out for the meeting; Diana had only agreed at all because she wanted to see if Reece Falcon would actually have the nerve to show himself as one of those 'executives'.

She wasn't in the least impressed by the expensive décor on the top floor of the Carlton building—thick-pile carpet in an attractive shade of pink, and ultra-modern white furnishings.

But she was impressed by the fact that she was to meet with Babs Carlton herself. The lady was a legend in her own lifetime, had taken over the ailing company after her husband's death seven years ago and turned it—with the financial backing of Reece Falcon—into a multi-million-pound success. Not being a social person, Diana had never had chance to meet the other woman, but had heard the business world lauding her ability. Reece must be very determined indeed to involve this very busy lady in his schemes!

The woman who stood up behind the huge glass-topped desk as Diana was ushered in by her secretary came as something of a shock to Diana: Barbara! Good God, it had never occurred to her that *Babs* Carlton could possibly be the lovely redhead Barbara whom Reece intended marrying!

Although the fact that she obviously was made
everything else make more sense now. Reece had in-
vested a considerable amount of money in Carlton
Cosmetics, and now that it was a multi-million-pound
concern he intended safeguarding that investment by
marrying his partner, Babs Carlton. He was even
making sure that Chris married the woman's daughter—Madeleine *Carlton*, she now realised too—so that
he was doubly insured!

It only took the minute or so for Babs Carlton to
walk round the side of her desk and hold out her hand
in greeting to Diana for Diana to realise all of this, and
she could only return the handshake dazedly. She had
thought Reece Falcon *couldn't* surprise her, but
this...!

'You're even more beautiful close to than you appeared in the Paris show,' Babs Carlton told her generously—generously, because this woman, even if she
hadn't heard the rumours of Diana's involvement with
Chris from another source, must have discussed the
relationship with Reece Falcon. Possibly post-coital.
God, Reece Falcon was incredible; how on earth had
he persuaded his future wife to offer her this prestigious contract with their company?

'Thank you,' Diana accepted smoothly as she sat
down, her control slowly returning, crossing one long
slender leg over the other, knowing the short fitted
black dress she had worn for the meeting showed off
their golden-tan length to perfection.

She had dressed this morning with the idea of seeing Reece Falcon in mind, but it was obvious, as Babs
Carlton resumed her seat behind the desk, that this
was to be a one-to-one meeting. Could she have been

mistaken after all? Diana frowned. Was Reece really not behind this offer? She had assumed his connection to the company was too much of a coincidence, but maybe she had been wrong about that; maybe it was Babs Carlton who, having seen her in Paris, had decided she was what the company needed for this promotion.

'Perhaps I could tell you a little about the new line we intend introducing this winter?' the other woman began briskly, very businesslike in the formal yellow suit with its black trim, her hair secured back at her nape with a tortoiseshell slide, looking a richer red in its confinement.

Diana could hardly conceal her disappointment at realising that Reece really wasn't involved in this. He really wasn't going to make any effort to see her again, which meant she had over-played her hand four weeks ago, moved too soon. And now it had all gone so terribly wrong.

'I don't think there's any point in that,' she told Babs Carlton dully, anxious to leave now, seeing little point in even continuing the meeting. 'I have made a point of never involving myself in the promotion of cosmetics.'

The other woman nodded calmly, not in the least perturbed by what she sensed was Diana's further rejection of the offer, although her eyes had narrowed calculatingly. 'That's precisely the reason we want you,' she explained lightly. 'You have made no secret of your views on animal experimentation to achieve beauty——'

'Then——'

'The new line we're introducing has been produced completely naturally,' the other woman told her with quiet triumph for having shot down that particular objection.

They were far from the first company to do this—most of the larger companies had realised the need for such a line and had hurried to provide the public with one. Carlton Cosmetics had obviously decided to join the market.

The fact that Babs Carlton was so familiar with Diana's feelings about make-up set off alarm bells inside her, and once again she had the feeling of someone else being behind all this. Reece Falcon. She was sure of it. Only *he* could come up with an offer like this that she was going to find it hard to refuse without prejudicing herself and her convictions! After years of protesting at cruelty to produce beauty products for women and men, she could hardly now turn down a chance to promote such a line from a reputable company like Carlton Cosmetics. Clever, clever Reece . . .

'I would need to know more about it,' she answered stiffly, knowing a grudging admiration for Reece's manipulation.

'Of course,' the other woman accepted smoothly. 'I expected as much.' She glanced at the slender watch on her wrist. 'Perhaps you would care to go with my assistant and meet some of the people dealing directly with the new line, and then join me for lunch afterwards?' she suggested lightly.

'I would like to see the new line,' Diana accepted non-committally.

To say she was impressed by everything she saw during the next hour was putting it mildly; Carlton Cosmetics had produced exactly the line of make-up, all bright colours and plenty of shine, that the market was crying out for—naturally produced, and not at incredibly high prices either. By the time she was taken back to Babs Carlton's office she knew it was going to be much harder than she had imagined to turn her back and walk away from this.

And still there had been no sign of Reece Falcon. When she had been so sure he was behind the offer her answer had been simple, cut and dried, but now——

'Ah, Diana.' He stood up smoothly from behind Babs Carlton's desk as she entered the office alone. 'Do join me,' he invited softly as she came to an abrupt halt in the doorway at seeing him there.

At last!

In some ways it was a relief to have her suspicions confirmed after all—almost a triumph, but in another way she knew she would be genuinely disappointed, now that she knew Reece Falcon *was* involved, not to be involved in the new make-up line after all. Because she had been verging on considering it, had been genuinely impressed by everything she had seen this morning.

Except Reece Falcon.

He had changed little in the last four weeks; he still wore his hand-made suit, a dark grey three-piece this time, with arrogant disregard for the elegance of its design, his hair cut meticulously short, his skin looking more tanned than ever, those grey eyes glittering silver as he met her gaze challengingly now.

Her hackles, as usual, rose just at the sight—and sound!—of him.

'I would rather not, thank you.' She shook her head, making no effort to move from the doorway. 'Perhaps you could thank Mrs Carlton for me, but——'

'Stop being so bloody stubborn and come in here and join me!' Reece had crossed the room in long strides even as she spoke, closing the door firmly behind her, dangerously close to her now as they both stood just inside the room. 'You are definitely the most stubborn,' he began exasperatedly, 'infuriating, *desirable* woman it has ever been my misfortune to meet!' This last came out as an agonised groan as his arms moved about her slenderness to mould her body to his while his lips lowered towards hers.

Every instinct in her body cried out in protest at the fierce demand of his mouth moving against her, but she forced herself not to push him away as she longed to do, knowing that if she attempted to do that she would only antagonise the situation. Let him realise for himself that she wasn't responding.

And she had *meant* to suffer his kiss in silence, to remain unmoved, and yet as the seconds passed and he showed no signs of his determination to elicit a response from her, any response, she knew it wasn't going to be as easy to do as she had thought.

Her body, too long denied any form of physical closeness, with anyone, was reacting instinctively, melting in the warmth of a human embrace. How long since anyone had held her, gathered her into the closeness of their warmth? Oh, there had been men over the years who would have been only too pleased to hold her like this, make love to her, but she knew, deep inside her, that if she ever allowed the warmth of another human being to penetrate the protective shell she had built around her emotions she might never recover from the vulnerability that would ensue.

The one man she had been sure would *never* breach that barrier had been Reece Falcon!

But perhaps, after all, he was the *only* person who could... Oh, God, she groaned inwardly as her slenderness curved instinctively against the hard muscles of his body, her lips softening and flowering beneath the insistent demand of his, his hands travelling the length of her body now with a sureness that made her tremble. She had to stop this. Now!

But it seemed she had no will left to do that, her throat arching now as the hard warmth of his lips moved caressingly down the pulsing column there, burning a path of desire in their wake, Diana trembling at this assault on her senses.

'Let's skip lunch and go back to my apartment,' Reece spoke gruffly against her earlobe, his own body pulsing his need. 'Or your flat,' he amended as he felt her instantly begin to withdraw from him. 'I don't give a damn which—I just want to be alone with you!'

Maybe if he hadn't spoken, if she hadn't heard the sound of his voice—but he did, and she had! And she thanked God that he had; his hold of sensuality was broken now, allowing her to realise exactly what she had been allowing to happen between them—worse, she had been responding! But that voice, the voice that had haunted her nightmares for years, both awake and asleep, had broken the spell he had weaved about her emotions.

She pulled sharply away from him, too shaken by her own ragged emotions at that moment to hide the contempt she felt for him as she looked into the dark, rugged beauty of his face.

But as his eyes narrowed she realised she should have been more careful about hiding that disgust—Reece was too astute a man not to realise there was something very wrong about her behaviour now after she had responded to him so naturally seconds ago. This man was no fool, and she had to remember that, must never be deceived into thinking otherwise, no matter what the provocation. And it was her own pride, a disgust at herself, that had given her that momentary lapse.

She thought quickly to cover her mistake—for mistake it had assuredly been—that narrowed, steely gaze studying her searchingly now. 'This office, *Barbara* Carlton's office, is hardly the place for this,' she told him coldly, deciding attack had to be her best form of defence—until she was more in control of her own betraying emotions!

His expression remained woodenly unchanged. 'That was why I suggested we leave,' he reminded her quietly.

'I didn't mean *that*,' Diana returned impatiently as he misunderstood her, her cheeks still flushed, her eyes wide green pools of disturbed emotion. 'As your fiancée, Mrs Carlton is obviously——'

'As my *what*?' Reece cut in incredulously.

It was Diana's turn to look at him searchingly now, his utter surprise at her statement perfectly obvious. So obvious that she knew she must have made a mistake...

She didn't know how she had, not when he had told
Charles in Paris that he wanted the wedding gown she
was modelling for his bride—— But had he actually
said it was for *his* bride? she suddenly realised. Now
that she thought back to the conversation, he had only
said *the* bride. But Barbara Carlton had been the
woman with him in Paris, she was sure of it.

She shook her head; none of this made any sense
any more.

Reece looked at Diana in total amazement. Barbara,
his *fiancée*?

Barbara was a beautiful woman, and he admitted
that five years ago, when they first met, the two of
them had indulged in an affair. But even then they had
both known exactly what they were doing, and what
each of them wanted from the relationship—for
Barbara a physical closeness with someone who understood the other demands she had in her life, with
Carlton Cosmetics to run, and a thirteen-year-old
daughter to bring up alone. Reece had comfortably
accepted those demands upon her time and emotions;
in fact it had suited him too that the relationship didn't
ask for more of him, that the two of them had a mutual respect for each other's abilities, as well as an attraction to each other.

But marriage? God, the thought had never entered
his head after the disaster he had made of things the
first time around, and he doubted it had entered
Barbara's either. In fact, he was sure it hadn't.

Reece knew, and accepted, that it was in his arrogant nature to despise the weakness of failure, and he
certainly made a point of never repeating his mistakes. He couldn't begin to understand how Diana had

ever jumped to the conclusion—because 'jumped' she certainly had!—that Barbara was to be his wife—that initial physical relationship between himself and Barbara was over long ago, although they still liked and respected each other, especially in a business capacity. In fact, Barbara had looked at him with knowing amusement when he had told them he wanted the model Divine for their new publicity campaign, passing a cutting remark about 'following in his son's footsteps—or did she mean bedrooms?'!

Reece's mouth thinned as he remembered that latter comment; he didn't want to think about the depth—or otherwise—of Chris's relationship with Diana. For the first time in his life he was aware of the emotion jealousy, and it was an emotion he felt weakened him when he would rather have been strong.

As for Barbara's mockery about his interest in the model Divine, Barbara was as aware as he that he actually owned fifty-one per cent of Carlton Cosmetics, while Barbara remained as working figurehead of the company; in other words, Barbara could bitch all she wanted, but at the end of the day it would be Reece's word that counted.

Although, in the circumstances, Barbara was entitled to feel a certain amount of apprehension about involving Divine with the company; it had been Diana's friendship with Chris that had threatened Chris and Madeleine's marriage plans, those same wedding plans he had discussed so amiably with Cathy in New York only—— Ah!

'Your fiancée,' Diana repeated at his incredulity, uncertainly this time, obviously realising she had made some sort of mistake.

He shook his head, in control of the situation again. For a few minutes, when she had looked at him so contemptuously a short time ago, he had thought he must have imagined her response when he held her in his arms. But if all this time she had thought he was engaged to marry another woman—God, she must have thought he and Chris both made a habit of indulging in extra-relationship affairs!—no wonder she held herself so aloof from him. He couldn't wait now to melt her defences completely!

'Barbara is a friend and business associate,' Reece clarified firmly. 'But she is also Madeleine's mother, and we were all in Paris together because *Madeleine* wanted to see the show. After Chris's tardy treatment of her in the preceding weeks, taking the two ladies to Paris seemed like the least I could do,' he added drily. 'Of course Madeleine was curious to see you too,' he grimaced. 'Which is probably the reason she decided, contrarily, that she had to have the wedding gown you modelled that evening, when she married Chris.' He shook his head disgustedly. 'Women!'

Diana still frowned. 'Madeleine . . .?'

He nodded confidently. 'She was with me that night too, sitting on my other side,' he supplied impatiently when Diana still looked puzzled.

Her brow cleared slightly at this explanation. 'The blonde . . .' she finally sighed.

Reece shrugged. 'Madeleine is a blonde, yes,' he confirmed dismissively. 'She was the one who wanted the Oxley wedding gown. For when she marries Chris,' he repeated pointedly, still not too sure of the state of Diana's own relationship with Chris, although remembering her outrage a few minutes ago, when she thought he was an engaged man kissing her, he really couldn't believe she and Chris had any more than friendship now. He *had* to believe that!

But, even if there hadn't been a Madeleine in Chris's life, he knew now that he could never have allowed Chris to marry Diana; he couldn't see himself spending the rest of his life lusting after his own daughter-in-law!

And each time he saw Diana he wanted her more. Almost five weeks now since he had last seen her, and rather than moving on from that initial fierce attraction he had felt towards her he had become even more obsessed with making her his than he had been before! She had to be his. *Had* to be.

And yet he still knew, as surely as how much he wanted her, that she was going to turn down the offer Carlton Cosmetics had made her...

The young blonde girl sitting at Reece's other side that night...! Diana hadn't known, hadn't realised—— She couldn't even remember the girl properly now, had only registered offhandedly that a redhead sat one side of that empty seat and a blonde on the other. *That* had been Madeleine, Chris's fiancée.

It was no surprise, then, knowing of Chris's relationship with Divine, that the other girl had decided she had to have that particular wedding dress.

And now that she knew Madeleine was the bride she could see that Reece wasn't on the point of marrying Barbara Carlton. That knowledge changed things, changed them considerably.

'I was mistaken,' she accepted with a cool inclination of her head.

'But…?' Reece prompted softly, watching her with intensely narrowed eyes.

She gave an acknowledging smile at his astuteness. '*But* I still have no intention of going anywhere with you when I leave this office!'

He shrugged dismissively, as if he had already guessed that. 'Not even lunch?' he persuaded.

'There would be little point in that,' Diana replied coolly, her emotions firmly under control again now, even more so now that she was aware of Barbara Carlton's true place in his life. 'I would just be wasting your time——'

'Oh, I doubt that,' he murmured softly.

The steadiness of her gaze told him exactly what she thought of his suggestive tone. 'I hope the new Carlton Cosmetics line is a success.' She picked up her clutchbag in preparation of leaving. 'I really do.'

'But you have no intention of being involved in its launch,' he drawled derisively.

'None at all,' she confirmed drily, turning away dismissively.

She had almost reached the door when she felt him grasp her arm and pull her back around to face him, his calm of a few seconds ago completely erased, his face twisted with anger. 'Don't turn your back on me!' he grated furiously.

She shrugged, unwilling to show him how much his hold on her arm was hurting her. 'The days of someone backing out of a room, bowing subserviently, are long gone, Reece,' she told him tauntingly. 'But if that's the sort of behaviour you ask for in an employee it's as well I turned down the offer to work for

Carlton Cosmetics!' She looked at him with cool green eyes.

Reece's fingers dropped abruptly away from her arm. 'Damn you, you know that wasn't what I—— What do you want from me, Diana?' he demanded with frustrated anger. '*What?*'

'Want from you?' she repeated lightly, knowing it was still too soon to tell him that. 'You don't have anything I want, Mr Falcon,' she told him derisively, her eyes mocking.

'You respond to me, damn it,' he bit out between clenched teeth, eyes glittering furiously.

'Absolutely nothing I want,' she said softly.

For a moment he looked as if he might actually strike her, and then he brought himself under control again, his hands clenching into fists at his sides. 'Get out of here,' he told her savagely. 'Before I do something we'll both regret!'

She raised her brows challengingly. 'Do *you* ever regret anything, Reece?' she asked huskily.

'I regret ever meeting you!' he told her frustratedly.

Finally, with a little half-smile of satisfaction, Diana left.

Reece Falcon was going to regret meeting her a lot more before this was finished!

CHAPTER SIX

'MY GOD, you look awful,' Chris told Reece cheer-
fully as he walked past the latter on the way into his
luxury penthouse apartment, Reece having opened the
door to him a few seconds earlier.

Reece followed him through to the sitting-room at
a more leisurely pace. 'Thanks for that vote of confidence from my nearest and dearest!' he returned ac-
idly.

Chris gave a dismissive shrug before dropping down
into one of the deep armchairs. 'I'm only telling you
the same thing your mirror must every time you look
in it to shave—although——' he looked up frowningly at his father '—that doesn't look as if it's been
too often, lately, by the look of you. What have you
been doing with yourself?' He pulled a face at his
father's less than immaculate appearance.

Reece sighed his impatience with the criticism; as
Chris so rightly pointed out, he could see every time
he looked in a mirror just how awful he looked! But
it had been a long week, and he certainly didn't need
this. 'Absolu—precisely nothing,' he corrected
abruptly as he realised what he had been about to say;
he didn't need any reminding of Diana and the things
she had said to him last week.

Chris gave him a disparaging look. 'Well, if this is what doing nothing does for you I recommend you stop it immediately!'

He looked like hell, he knew he did. He had lost weight, he had dark shadows under his eyes from lack of sleep, a grey pallor to his skin. But the way that he looked was nowhere near as bad as he *felt*.

During those first few weeks after meeting Diana, when he had tried to stay away from her, he had filled in his time doing all the things he usually enjoyed, spent time with dozens of women who if not as beautiful as Diana, were at least more amenable. And he had worked sometimes until he just collapsed into bed at night too tired to do anything but sleep. And none of that had erased Diana from his thoughts. This time, with no choice but to stay away from her—she had made it more than clear she didn't want to see him again!—he had decided to take a week off work and just stay at his apartment, read some of the books he had been stockpiling away for when he eventually found time to read them, watch a little television, a few videos. And after a week of that he was climbing the walls, going quietly insane—and no nearer getting over his obsession with Diana than he had been a week ago!

'What a comfort you are to me, Chris!' He grimaced his derision.

His son looked unrepentent. 'Would you rather I lied and told you how well you're looking?'

'I would rather you weren't here at all—— Oh never mind!' Reece dismissed impatiently, throwing himself down into the armchair opposite Chris, wearing denims and a loose shirt, his feet bare in the thick pile carpet. 'What do you want, Chris?'

His son grimaced. 'No one, apparently, has seen or heard from you the last week, so I thought I had better come over and make sure you're still alive!'

He raised dark brows derisively. 'It took you long enough!'

Chris shrugged unconcernedly. 'I didn't realise until yesterday that you hadn't been into the office——'

'Not having been in yourself either, I suppose,' Reece guessed shrewdly, knowing by Chris's unrepentant grin that he was right.

'There have to be some perks to being the boss's son,' Chris shrugged. 'So I took a week off to spend time with Maddy.'

'How are things between the two of you now?' Reece's eyes were narrowed questioningly, although Chris certainly looked cheerful enough. Although that wasn't that reassuring, now that he thought about it— Chris had looked cheerful when he'd imagined himself in love with Diana too!

'Fine,' Chris dismissed carelessly. 'When I told Maddy you had taken the unprecedented step of having a week's holiday, and then hidden yourself away here from everyone, she agreed with me that perhaps you were sick and we should——'

'Very funny, Chris,' he sighed wearily, tiring of this game. 'I took a week off because I needed one——'

'You've needed one for years,' his son put in drily. 'Why the sudden need now?'

'You and Maddy decided you should...?' He ignored this probing question and posed one of his own.

Chris looked at him searchingly for several long seconds, receiving only a blank stare in return for his concern, shrugging resignedly as he realised he was wasting his time pushing the point any further. 'We decided to take pity on one of the old folk and invite you out to a party with us this evening,' he grinned.

Reece smiled in spite of himself. Chris really was the most infuriating of sons—he had no right coming here cheering him up when he was determined to wallow in misery! And yet he had to admit, to himself at least, he already felt better than he had for days.

Chris sat forward in his chair, sensing his father's weakening attitude. 'Do come with us,' he encouraged gruffly, all humour gone now. 'Barbara said if she can get away she might join us later too.'

Maybe this *was* what he needed—a night out with people he could relax with; too often, when he was with people, he had to remember he was Reece Falcon, and that more often than not the people he came into contact with had an angle for wanting to meet him. Years of knowing that, of having to accept it as a fact of his life, had warped his way of dealing with people.

Diana hadn't had an angle, hadn't even wanted to meet him, certainly hadn't wanted to be with him—— Oh, damn Diana!

'All right, I'll come,' he told Chris more forcefully than he might otherwise have done if thoughts of Diana hadn't intruded once again. But just thinking about her was enough to upset him nowadays. He needed an evening out where he could just forget about her completely.

*   *   *

Almost the first person he saw when he got to the party a couple of hours later was Diana...!

And she wasn't alone!

Diana saw Reece across the room almost at the same moment he spotted her.

These sort of parties—loud music, noisy chatter competing with that music, the conversation consisting mainly of what people had or hadn't got, where they were going or had been on their latest trip abroad, who was having an affair with whom—were exactly the sort of evening Diana hated the most! But Charles had asked her to accompany him so that she could wear one of his gowns, so it was actually a night of work for her.

It wasn't surprising that Reece had spotted her so easily—she was a blaze of colour in a gown that was red at the throat and then passed through all the shades down to orange at its above-knee-length hem!

She had seen and heard nothing from Reece Falcon again during this last week, and yet here he was tonight. And as he scowled across the room at her she didn't think he was particularly pleased to see her here; indeed he tensed defensively as he excused himself from Chris—and Maddy?—to cross the room towards her with determined strides.

His eyes were glittering dangerously by the time he reached her side. 'What's the relationship between you and Oxley?' he demanded unexpectedly.

Ah. She could breathe again. For a brief moment she had thought he might have found out. 'Professional respect,' she answered coolly, glancing briefly across to where Charles was deep in conversation with a woman who wanted him to design a gown specifically for her.

'And?' Reece grated, his mouth a thin line of displeasure.

'I enjoy working for him,' she added pointedly, knowing her shaft had gone home as Reece's eyes narrowed coldly. 'I'm working for him tonight, as it happens,' she explained lightly, knowing that if she continued to constantly rebuff this man it would, ultimately, result in the exact opposite of what she actually wanted to happen. A little sugar among the vinegar...

'You are?' He sounded a little uncertain now, some of the anger leaving his face.

'I am.' She allowed herself a smile. 'Is that Maddy with Chris?' She looked across the room at the young couple as they stood together talking.

Reece easily followed her line of vision. 'Yes,' he confirmed unnecessarily. 'And things seem to have stabilised between them again,' he added harshly. 'So stay away from them tonight!'

He still wasn't sure about her own relationship with Chris, Diana realised; Chris was certainly extracting his pound of flesh from that situation. He was probably still furious with his father for his interference!

Lips painted the same vivid shade of red as the top of the gown she wore curved into a smile. 'I couldn't possibly ignore Chris all night.' She shook her head. 'Most of the people here tonight know we're friends, and it would just look——'

'I didn't ask you to ignore him,' Reece cut in irritably. 'Only that you don't play cat-and-mouse games with him in front of Maddy.'

Diana looked at the other girl consideringly. Madeleine Carlton looked young, yes, but she was also a very self-possessed young woman; as the daughter of Barbara Carlton, and with a finishing-school education so recently behind her, she was bound to be. Tall—although not as tall as Diana—with shoulder-length blonde hair she wore in a straight style, Maddy wore her black designer gown—not an Oxley!—with youthful elegance.

No, Diana didn't believe Reece's concern was for this young girl at all; she felt sure that his worry was much closer to home—namely himself!

She turned back to him. 'Maddy looks more than capable of standing up for herself,' she said drily.

He relaxed slightly, darkly attractive in a lightly patterned dark grey shirt and grey fitted trousers, the latter moulded to the lean length of his legs. Although, Diana realised as she gave him a closer look, he seemed more strained than when she had last seen him—paler, lines beside his eyes from lack of sleep. Because of her...? God, she hoped so!

'She is,' he confirmed ruefully. 'Would you like a drink?' he suggested as a waiter passed them with a laden tray of filled glasses of what looked like champagne.

She glanced across to where Charles was still deep in conversation with his client, the two of them obviously still discussing the new design the lady would like; Diana knew from experience that work was the only thing that could so engross Charles!

Diana turned back to Reece again. 'Why not?' she accepted with a shrug, her face remaining impassive as she saw the look of triumph that blazed momentarily

in silver-coloured eyes before it was quickly masked
again. Yes, a little sugar was definitely in order just
now...

It was inevitable that, drinks in hand, they should
drift over to where Chris and Madeleine were indulging in a lightly flirtatious conversation, although Chris
seemed happy enough to forgo that to turn and hug
Diana, kissing her warmly on the lips as he did so. She
allowed him the liberty—and liberty they both knew
it was!—because it suited her, for the moment, as
much as it did him, to keep his father slightly off-
balance. Although she wasn't too sure about
Madeleine...!

'It's just as well I'm not the jealous type.' Maddy
was the one to interrupt their greeting.

Diana looked across at her curiously, not immune
to the hard glitter in the steady blue gaze. It was obvious as she looked at the young girl, now that she was
aware of their connection, of the relationship between Babs Carlton and Madeleine—there was a slight
facial similarity, especially around the eyes—and
Maddy, for all her youth, like her mother, was no fool!
It only needed the example of her handling of Chris
during his brief infatuation with Diana to know that;
most women in that situation would have screamed
and shouted, thrown a tantrum of some sort, but
Madeleine had simply sat back and waited for the infatuation to burn itself out. As she had known it
would. Possibly because she knew she had something
much more alluring to Chris, in the long run, than the
simple attraction to a beautiful face! Although perhaps that was being unfair to the other girl; Madeleine

and Chris certainly did seem to have a closeness between them that spoke of genuine love.

'Just as well,' Diana echoed drily, the two women sharing a look of mutual understanding. It was a look that said Diana knew she had only borrowed Chris for a short time, Maddy's in return telling her that although she had been worried for a while in the end it had perhaps turned out for the best, that Chris was all the more attentive and loving because of his lapse. It was a look that also said the two of them would probably even become friends one day!

Reece saw the look that passed between the two women and marvelled at it; did this beautiful woman cast a spell over *everyone* she met?

Even Barbara, experienced and somewhat cynical after years in the cosmetics business, had been impressed by the cool beauty of the model Divine, had been truly disappointed, even knowing of her friendship with Chris and the danger that could represent to her own daughter's happiness, when Reece told her of the model's adamant decision in not being involved with their publicity campaign.

What was it about Diana that made men and women alike gravitate to her cool loveliness?

If he knew the answer to that, perhaps he would be able to sleep again at night!

Chris stood next to Diana now, his arm about the slenderness of her waist, and Reece scowled as he saw the familiarity. Madeleine might not be showing any jealousy, but Reece knew he wasn't faring quite so well. He wanted to strangle his own son with his bare hands!

'Great party, hmm, Dad?'

Reece looked up to find Chris watching him speculatively. And the last thing he needed right now was for Chris to get 'speculative' about his behaviour towards Diana—Chris could be an absolute pain when he decided to start making mischief! Equally undesirable would be Chris's fury over Reece's own attraction to the woman he had so disapproved of for him. Oh, hell! The sooner he could get Cathy over here to help organise Chris and Madeleine's wedding, as they had discussed her doing, the better; it might take Chris's mind off Reece and Diana. Might . . .

He straightened now. 'I haven't even had chance to talk to our hostess yet,' he rasped. 'If you'll excuse me.' He strode away from the potentially explosive situation. For possibly the first time in his life he walked away.

He was having a lot of firsts since Diana Lamb had entered his life!

'You were right about your father, Chris,' Maddy said slowly once he had gone, staring after him. 'He doesn't seem at all like himself.' She frowned worriedly.

'No,' Chris acknowledged thoughtfully, moving away from Diana, his gaze suddenly levelled questioningly on her.

She returned that gaze unflinchingly. 'Has your father been ill?' she enquired politely.

'Not exactly,' Chris replied slowly, still looking at her searchingly. 'More—behaving out of character,' he enlarged thoughtfully.

As far as Diana could see Reece Falcon was still acting completely *in* character, having arrogantly issued her an instruction and then expected it to be obeyed without question! But she couldn't deny she was curious about this 'out of character' behaviour of his...

She gave a dismissive shrug. 'Men his age do tend to do that sort of thing, I've heard.' She was deliberately provocative.

'Men his age?' Maddy repeated with a puzzled frown.

Diana nodded, her expression completely deadpan. 'Middle-aged crisis. It can happen to a lot of men approaching forty. I've heard it can be quite—disturbing for the family of the man afflicted,' she added conversationally.

For several seconds the other couple just looked at her in stunned silence for what she had just said, and then, as she raised her brows in mocking humour, both Chris and Maddy burst into laughter. Diana couldn't help grinning herself at this conspiratorial humour at Reece's expense, although the smile faded from her lips as she turned slightly and found a fierce silver gaze fixed on her angrily from across the room, almost as if Reece knew he was the reason for their laughter.

'Middle-aged crisis!' Maddy repeated with a chuckle. 'My God, anyone less likely to be suffering from the inadequacy that causes that than Reece, I have yet to meet!'

'Oh, I don't know...' Chris drawled speculatively.

Diana wrenched her gaze away from Reece's to look at Chris, only to find he was watching her in return, brows raised in mocking question. She could see that he was wondering now at the possible reason for his father's unpredictability.

'No, I don't believe that can be it.' Maddy shook her head with certainty. 'Not Reece. It has to be something else that's bothering him.'

'Or someone,' Chris put in softly.

'It's probably something to do with work,' Maddy dismissed, not picking up on the undertones of Chris's conversation at all. 'Mummy tells me you turned down a contract with Carlton Cosmetics,' she said, turning to Diana curiously. 'I hope your decision didn't have anything to do with Chris and me...?'

A *very* self-possessed young lady, Diana acknowledged again admiringly. Chris was going to have his work cut out with this clever young lady. Madeleine had obviously been 'finished' in grand style in Switzerland!

'Not at all,' Diana replied smoothly. 'I never do that sort of work.'

The other girl frowned. 'I thought all the top models were after cosmetics contracts nowadays, that it was the way to really make their name?'

'Divine believes in doing what you feel right about,' Chris told her lightly. 'That if she——' He broke off awkwardly as he suddenly seemed to realise he was being decidedly indelicate quoting Diana's beliefs to his fiancée. Colour slowly darkened his cheeks as Maddy looked at him with derisively raised brows.

'As I was saying,' she drawled pointedly before turning back to Diana. 'Surely a contract like the one offered to you is where the big money is in modelling?' she frowned interestedly.

'Diana believes there are more important things in life than money,' drawled a mocking voice.

Diana slowly turned to look at Reece, having been completely unaware of his presence there until he spoke, but knowing as she looked at him that his taunt had been deliberate—and that he didn't really believe she meant that at all. She moved slightly to one side to allow him into their group. 'If I didn't believe that, I would have accepted Carlton Cosmetics' offer,' she pointed out mildly.

'Maybe,' he shrugged. 'Or maybe you just have a more lucrative offer in mind.'

Diana eyed him pityingly for the explanation he had come up with in his own mind for her refusal of the offer; he really didn't have any other value in his life than money and the power it gave him. But then, she had always known that. Any man, businessman or not, with the sort of wealth Reece Falcon had, had no need to push another man to the desperate extreme of taking his own life just to give him more money and possessions. *Unless* he was Reece Falcon...!

And he had obviously looked for, and believed he had found, the only explanation he could understand for her refusal of the Carlton Cosmetic contract.

She shrugged. 'It wouldn't necessarily have to be more lucrative,' she told him quietly.

His mouth twisted with derision. 'Just something you "feel right about"?' he scorned.

He had obviously been listening to their conversation for some time before speaking up himself—although Diana doubted he had heard her disparaging remarks about mid-life crisis; he would be a lot more cutting with her if he had, she was sure. 'Not even that,' she said calmly. 'Carlton's new range of cosmetics sounds exactly what I approve of.'

'Then——'

'But when, or if, I become involved in a contract like that,' she continued firmly over his interruption, 'it will have to be one that I didn't think *you* were instrumental in arranging!' Her head went back proudly as she issued the challenge.

Madeleine could be heard drawing in a sharp breath, and Chris's eyes widened incredulously—it obviously hadn't even occurred to him that there was such a connection between the contract offer and his father. But now it did. And, considering how strongly against her his father had been at their last meeting, he was now realising how odd it was that the contract had been offered at all!

Diana looked at Reece, seeing the mixed emotions on his darkly arrogant face—the admiration he felt for the directness of her challenge, irritation that she had chosen to issue it in front of an audience. And such an interested audience!

So she *had* known it was him behind the offer and not just Carlton Cosmetics, Reece acknowledged impatiently. Well, he had wanted to know—and she had certainly told him! But so much more than he had really wanted to know, and in front of Chris and Madeleine too. Would this woman never cease annoying him? He had a feeling the answer to that was no!

'Is that really the only reason you refused the contract?' His intent gaze didn't leave the cool beauty of her face for a second.

She gave an inclination of her head. 'Of course.'

Straight for the jugular. No nonsense. As sharp as a dagger. And the result was he just wanted her more!

'In business it pays never to let emotions play any part in the decisions you make,' he drawled dismissively. 'Evaluate the situation and act on it,' he shrugged, frowning concernedly as he saw her reaction to his words. All the colour seemed to have drained out of her face, and her eyes were wide and haunted, deepening in colour now until they almost looked black. What the hell——?

That he had somehow said the wrong thing he had no doubt, that he had touched on some personal pain he also didn't doubt. That Diana could display such fierceness of emotion set him back on his heels! She was always so composed, so much in control, that he also despised himself for being the one to cause her pain now, but at the same time he could only welcome *any* show of emotion other than that coldness she usually showed him.

But he wondered about the pain he saw in her eyes now, at what had caused it. He knew that a model's life, unless she was at the top of her profession as Diana now was, could be a hard one, realised that during the early years, as in any other business, it could be difficult to know whom to trust and whom not to trust. And young girls looking for fame and fortune were always the ripest for being cheated and taken advantage of. Somewhere, in the last four years of her career, Diana must have known just such a painful experience.

And Reece wanted to strangle the man responsible for hurting her!

'There was no emotion involved in my decision concerning Carlton Cosmetics,' she told him now harshly, her cheeks still waxy-pale. 'It was cut and dried from the onset. I only attended the meeting because my agent asked me to. You *are* Carlton Cosmetics.' She looked at him unblinkingly.

Reece returned that gaze searchingly, and saw, for all her pallor, that she was back in control again now. If she had ever lost it. Which he was no longer sure about.

What he *was* sure of was that he was sick of the situation that existed between him and this woman. He would have his say where she was concerned once and for all, and then if necessary—God, how he hoped it wouldn't be!—he would move on. He had always known in the past when to cut his losses and go on, and Diana Lamb had disrupted his well-ordered life enough already...!

CHAPTER SEVEN

DIANA could feel the nausea receding now, the waves of dizziness that had almost made her believe, for a few seconds, that she was going to totally disgrace herself and collapse in the middle of this crowded room!

That remark about emotions had been so totally Reece Falcon, was the exact attitude that had destroyed her father, and it had shaken her to the very roots of her being. God, how she hated this man and all he stood for!

She couldn't carry on with this charade any longer; she had to get it over with.

'I'm sorry, Reece.' She put a hand up to her throbbing temple. 'I'm afraid I'm suddenly not feeling well; if I make my excuses to Charles, would you mind driving me home?'

She was too numbed of emotion at that moment to even mind the look of triumph that blazed in the glittering silver eyes at her request. God, she had to get over feeling this way before they reached her flat, otherwise these last painful weeks would all have been in vain. She would get over it—had to, had made a promise to herself and the memory of her father. And she had no intention of breaking it!

'Unless, of course,' she murmured with a frown as she saw Barbara Carlton enter the room, 'I would be taking you away from anyone...?' She should have realised he had arranged to meet someone at the party—if not Barbara then some other woman; after all, making up a threesome with his son and his son's fiancée wasn't usual for him! She arched speculative brows at him.

He had seen Barbara too now, his eyes narrowing as his gaze returned to Diana. 'No,' he told her firmly. 'You won't be taking me away from anyone or any-thing. I'm ready to leave whenever you are,' he added softly.

So he really had been telling the truth when he claimed there was nothing but a professional rela-tionship between himself and Barbara Carlton; he would hardly leave with her now if there was any-thing else between them. 'I'll just go and tell Charles we're leaving,' Diana nodded before looking at the young couple. 'It was nice to meet you at last, Maddy,' she said warmly.

The other girl smiled. 'Especially as Chris hadn't told you a *thing* about me!' she teased him.

'Oh, come on, you two.' Chris looked uncomfort-able again now. 'Give a man a break!'

Madeleine put her hand in the crook of his arm as she smiled up at him sweetly. 'I will, darling—if you ever decide to forget again that we're engaged. And I doubt a broken nose would look as distinguished on you as it does on Reece!'

Diana couldn't help but join the general laughter at Chris's expense. She admired Madeleine tremen-dously for the mature way she was handling Chris's lapse, and she could see from Chris's slightly dazed expression that he would be slightly wary in future of upsetting this kitten he seemed to have got by the tail, that he would think twice—three times!—before even considering forgetting he had a fiancée again. Diana doubted he would have got away with it the first time if Madeleine hadn't been in Switzerland, and she was sure the younger girl would be keeping a closer eye on him in future.

Charles raised his brows when Diana told him who was taking her home. 'Take care, Diana,' he frowned concernedly, glancing across the room to where Reece was now in conversation with Barbara. 'The man has a reputation——'

'I know.' Diana squeezed his hand, grateful for his concern, all the more so because she knew it was of a paternal kind and not because of any interest in her himself; he and Joanna had been living together for years. 'Don't worry,' she smiled. 'I can take care of myself.' Because she had been doing it for years, had had no one else there to take care of her. And she had Reece Falcon to thank for that.

Charles had no reason to worry about her; she wasn't the one in any danger...

Reece was genuinely sorry Diana wasn't feeling well, and although it wasn't the best circumstance to be alone with her he was grateful for the opportunity anyway. Maybe now wasn't the best time to tell her how he felt about her, but God knew when would be the best time with this elusive woman!

He inwardly thanked whatever impulse had made him bring his own car tonight, although he had originally done it because he wanted the means to leave any time he wanted to without being accused of inconveniencing Chris and Madeleine. And when he had set out this evening he had believed he would want to leave very soon after he arrived; now, with Diana seated beside him in the darkness of the car, he felt as elated as a young schoolboy on his first date. What had she done to him?

They didn't speak as he drove unerringly back to her flat, both seeming lost in their own thoughts. And Reece realised, as the miles quickly passed, he was as *nervous* as a young schoolboy on his first date too!

Diana was well aware of the elation in the man sitting beside her. But it didn't bother her. He might think he had won this particular battle, but he still wasn't about to win the war. There wasn't going to be *any* victor in the war she was waging—they were all the losers.

'Would you like to come in for coffee?' she asked as he parked the car. 'It's the least I can offer you,' she added huskily, 'when I've dragged you away from the party.'

Reece's mouth twisted. 'I happen to hate those chatty, everyone-trying-to-impress-each-other type of parties! I only went at all because Chris and Madeleine asked me to. But I thought you weren't feeling well . . .?' He tilted his head questioningly.

Diana looked back at him in the glow given off by the street-lamp just outside the car. 'So you don't want coffee,' she nodded.

'I would love a coffee,' he told her firmly. 'If you're feeling well enough . . .?'

'I wouldn't have offered if I didn't,' Diana drawled.

'Then coffee it is,' he agreed, quickly climbing out of the car to come round and open her door for her.

Puddle, the traitor, twined himself in and out of Reece Falcon's legs in greeting once he had recognised who their visitor was, leaving several black hairs on the dark grey trousers before wandering off again to settle himself back in the cosy bed Diana had made up for him near the window.

Secretly Diana had wished Puddle might have taken a dislike to Reece, then he would have shown his displeasure by sinking his teeth into his leg the way he did to her when she had been away. Fickle cat!

'There really is nothing between you and Oxley?' Reece spoke suddenly into the silence.

She met his gaze steadily. 'Would it really bother you if there were?'

Reece's mouth tightened. 'Is there?' he grated.

'No,' she sighed. 'Nothing at all. And there never has been either,' she answered the question she knew would come next. 'Reece, now who is playing games?' She quirked dark brows pointedly.

His eyes narrowed warily—like an animal that sensed it was being driven into a corner, Diana realised. And it was his own desire for her that was trapping him! Enigmatic didn't even begin to describe this man; he wanted her, made no secret of the fact, and yet he still resented his involvement with her. Perhaps that attitude wasn't so difficult to understand after all, not when she had told him so bluntly how uninterested she was in him. It was the fact that her attitude now seemed so different that was bothering him, she could tell. Most men would just have been grateful for that apparent change, but then, Reece Falcon wasn't 'most men'!

'Let me ask *you* something, Reece,' she said slowly, moistening red painted lips, not with any intention of being provocative but because they suddenly felt dry. But as the intensity of his silver gaze became fixed on the movement Diana knew Reece had reacted to it anyway. He might be wary, but that certainly didn't stop him wanting her! 'What do you want from me?' she asked softly.

He drew in a sharp breath at the directness of her question, taking his time formulating an answer.

But time was something Diana knew she could no longer give him. 'No more games from either of us, Reece.' She shook her head. 'I'm sure you must have realised by now that it isn't something I enjoy indulging in.' She gave a slightly derisive smile.

He shrugged. 'I'm not sure I know anything about you at all.' His eyes were narrowed. 'Who are you, Diana Lamb?'

Now it was her turn to catch her breath in her throat. 'What do you mean?' she finally managed to say, every nerve in her body tensed now.

He ran a hand over his brow in weary acceptance. 'Why do I find myself thinking about you all the time? Why do I want you so damned much?' he said harshly.

She was filled with elation at his admission, and didn't even protest when he swept her up into his arms and began to kiss her with a fierceness that bordered on savagery.

But it was such total and raw desire, beyond either of their control, Diana's head spinning at Reece's closeness, the hard lines of his body pressed against hers.

What happened next was *totally* out of her control, her arms moving up about Reece's neck, seemingly of their own volition, her lips flowering beneath his as they gentled to searching passion, sipping, tasting, drinking thirstily, his tongue a warm caress against her lips before venturing further, telling her of his need of her. And it was a need she could feel echoed in her own body, her back arching, a low groan escaping her throat as one of Reece's hands moved in a slow caress across her breast, the tip hardening instantly, a thumb-pad seeking, and immediately finding, that response.

Diana's legs felt weak, her body filled with sensations she had never even dreamt of experiencing for herself, a burning ache within her that she had no idea how to assuage. And it felt almost as if she would faint away completely as Reece's mouth left hers and his head lowered to gently draw her pulsing nipple into the warm cavern of his mouth through the thin material of her dress. For a fleeting moment—very fleeting!— she vaguely registered that Charles would be furious with her if his gown was damaged in any way, and then she didn't care how he felt as warmth and longing coursed through her limbs, couldn't have cared less if the gown had been ripped to shreds at her feet.

This wasn't the way it was meant to be—she wasn't supposed to respond to this man in this way!

But she couldn't stop her feelings, and knew she was lost completely as Reece's mouth returned search-ingly to hers, revelling in that passionate intensity.

'*This* is what I want!' he finally groaned low in his throat. 'You. Beside me. In bed. On the floor! Any damn where!' he rasped self-derisively.

That voice. Always it was the sound of that voice that brought her back to her senses, that reminded her of exactly who he was!

Diana looked at him with darkly bewildered eyes, knowing as she did so that she was *falling in love* with him, that it was only when he spoke, and she remembered who he was, that she knew it could never be between them.

She couldn't allow herself to fall in love with this man—to do so would destroy her!

She was going away from him again—Reece could sense it, even though physically she was still close to him, her body moulded against his. And he couldn't let her go away from him this time; he wanted the warmth and passion she had shown him a few minutes ago.

'Diana!' He shook her gently. 'Don't look at me like that. I want to make love to you, nothing more, but nothing less either!' he told her bluntly, knowing she had to be aware of his desire, the hardness of his body giving him away.

Damn, he had come so close, only to feel her withdrawing into herself once again. And he couldn't stand yet more weeks of hell, of denying himself this woman he wanted so much. Not when he knew she wanted him too. And she did want him. Reece knew that her response had been completely spontaneous a short time ago, that even she had been taken aback at the depth of her feeling.

'Diana!' He shook her again, his gaze fierce on the paleness of her face.

She swallowed hard. 'I—I've never had an affair, Reece,' she told him huskily.

He frowned his puzzlement at the statement. She couldn't mean—— 'What are you saying?' he demanded harshly.

She met his gaze unflinchingly. 'That I'm a virgin.'

Reece felt himself sway dizzily with elation. It was incredible to believe this beautiful woman-child, with her hauntingly lovely face and body, had never known a lover's touch, and never—despite all his agonising imaginings to the contrary—lain in the warmth of a man's arms in the aftermath of lovemaking. And yet he didn't doubt her words, was sure now that this was the reason she always seemed so elusive—because she was!

And as he looked into that coolly beautiful face, down the length of that sensually lovely body, he knew he didn't want any other man to possess her. Ever. He wanted her for himself.

That she wanted him too he didn't doubt now, but many men must have wanted her in the past, and it was inconceivable that she hadn't wanted any of them. Why hadn't she taken any of them as her lover? And then he berated himself for being so damned suspicious. Maybe it was because he had finally found everything he had ever wanted wrapped up in this hauntingly lovely woman—beauty, brains, no complicated past for him to accept and contend with, so that he just couldn't believe his luck in having found her at all.

'Marry me,' he heard himself say—to his own stunned surprise. Because until the words actually left his lips he hadn't even been aware he had been thinking of saying them. And maybe he hadn't—he didn't seem able to think straight at all when he was close to Diana!

He wasn't sure which one of them was the more shocked when she whispered, 'Yes!'

CHAPTER EIGHT

THE idea would probably never even have come to her if she hadn't been introduced to Christopher Falcon at a promotional dinner three months ago, hadn't seen how different the last twelve years had been for him, with his father's wealth behind him.

During her eight years at school after her father died Diana had felt only numb hatred for the man who was responsible for his death, the hatred becoming a gnawing ache when she left school and found a job and then constantly found herself looking at photographs of 'the successful Reece Falcon' in newspapers. But even then it had been a detached sort of hatred, her chances of meeting the man himself being very remote, even when her modelling career became so well established. Being introduced to Chris had changed all that, and she had realised that she finally had a chance to avenge her father's death, and in a way that would hit Reece Falcon the hardest.

She knew, from what she had read, and from what Chris had now told her of his father, that Reece loved his son very much. But still she didn't want to hurt Chris; her argument was with Reece Falcon. And it was the older man she had deliberately set out to captivate; she wanted him to know the same helplessness that her father had, to know how it felt to lose the person you loved above all things, as she had when her father had died.

Chris, she was sorry to say, had merely been her bait to attract Reece Falcon's attention to her. Because once she had his attention she had been sure her very elusiveness would act as a lure to a man who was accustomed to taking whatever and whoever he wanted.

Even now she couldn't believe how well she had succeeded, that Reece Falcon had actually proposed to her—and that she had accepted!

Reece gave a shaky laugh as he recovered slightly, his hands moving caressingly down her arms to clasp hers. 'I can't believe I just did that!' he said shakily.

Diana's eyes widened in alarm. Was he changing his mind already, regretting his impulsiveness?

God, wouldn't it be better if he did? Because all of this was backfiring on her, and she realised how poorly she had actually thought out what she was doing. Meeting Chris had been the catalyst to a set of moves she now realised would result in her subjecting herself to a living hell too as Reece's wife. She had to be slightly mad to have even thought of doing such a thing.

And then she had a vision of her father, his pain and anguish, the way she had last seen him, the blood—oh, God, the blood!

That silent scream after she had seen him dead had gone on for months and months, the deep emotional trauma of what she had seen meaning she couldn't have spoken even if she had wanted to. But she hadn't wanted to. It was easier to stay cocooned inside herself rather than be expected to talk about her father, about seeing him dead. And all that had happened because of Reece Falcon.

But she was falling in love with the man! How could that be? She didn't have any answer to that anguished question; she only knew it was happening.

'Hey, I didn't say I regretted it,' Reece cajoled as he saw the paleness of her cheeks. 'Only that I can't believe it.'

She shook her head, frightened of her own emotions now. How could she possibly think of marrying this man, loving him and hating him at the same time?

Reece was starting to look really worried now at her continued silence. 'It will be all right, Diana,' he told her firmly. 'I'll *make* it all right,' he promised her. 'Only now that I've proposed and you've said yes, for God's sake don't ask for time to think it over or I shall really be worried!'

That was exactly what she had been going to do!

She felt as if she were waking after a long nightmare, emerging out of the deep, dark tunnel she had existed in since her father's death, an unemotional cushion that, while protecting her, had also kept her completely removed from love as well as pain. And Reece Falcon was breaking down all those barriers that had protected her for so long...

God, she *had* fallen in love with the one man who should have been her enemy—should have been? Was!

How could she love and hate him at the same time? Or was it true that there was a very thin line between love and hate? She had never thought, in her wildest of imaginings, that she would fall in love with Reece Falcon! That possibility hadn't entered into her plans at all.

What should she do now? She couldn't marry
him—loving him as she did, she would be subjecting
herself to a life of misery. But how could she *not*
marry him, loving him as she did? How would she live
without him now?

'Diana, I know we've only just met,' Reece spoke
forcefully as he sensed her indecision, his hands tight-
ening painfully on hers. 'That we've done nothing but
argue since we did meet,' he added ruefully. 'But
sometimes an instantaneous attraction can do that. At
least——' he grimaced '—I think it can. This has never
happened to me before either!'

No, she could see that it hadn't; she knew that this
self-confident, arrogantly assured man had been
knocked slightly off-balance ever since they'd first
met. But everything was all muddled in her mind now.
She had meant, on their wedding day, to present him
with who she really was, to make him realise exactly
who he was making his wife, who her father was. But
she no longer wanted to do that now, not in that way,
not in triumph. But Reece was going to find out who
her father was anyway as soon as he realised her name
wasn't actually Diana Lamb, and once he knew that he
was going to realise, with his intelligence, exactly why
she had behaved in the way she had these last weeks.
It was all going to rebound on her with sickening re-
percussions; *she* was going to be the one destroyed,
not him . . .

Reece watched her anxiously as the different emotions flickered across her face. And he could see from
her expression, as it had been with him, until he had
actually proposed and she had accepted, that it had

been the last thing she had thought would happen to-night, that she was as shocked by the commitment she had just made as he was that he had asked for it!

Good God, he had thought he would never marry again, that he liked his life the way that it was. Or, at least, he had ... This last five weeks, since first meeting Diana, he had come to realise just how empty his life actually was, to know an ache inside himself for something more, for something—he hadn't known what. Now he knew that hunger was for Diana, wanting her to be his wife.

But at the same time he realised he was older than her, and not just by eighteen years, but also in experience: he had a failed marriage behind him and a son not much younger than she was. He had never realised until this moment just what a bad matrimonial catch he was; he had always thought—— But he had *never* thought of remarrying before, had known after things went so badly wrong with Cathy that there were certain things he couldn't give to a marriage. But he wanted Diana so badly, so desperately, that he knew he would have to deceive her until after they were married. He had so much else to give her, surely that one thing——

He quickly put the torment from his mind, determined to deal with Diana's uncertainties once and for all; she would be his!

'I suggest we arrange the wedding for as soon as possible,' he told her arrogantly, his gaze challenging as her eyes widened in protest. 'There's no reason to wait.'

'I have work commitments for months ahead,' she put in huskily.

He hated the idea of his wife 'strutting her stuff' for the great general public, as he had so crudely thought it that first night in Paris. But at the same time he realised he was going to have to tread very warily with this young woman; if he pushed her too far she was likely to take flight. Hadn't she already shown him very effectively how determined *she* could be? There would be time later—once they were safely married!—to tell her exactly how he felt about her career.

'Then we'll work our wedding—and honeymoon——' God, he felt weak at the knees at the thought of their honeymoon! '—around them.'

Diana shook her head. 'Now that we've made the decision, there's no hurry——'

'Isn't there?' Reece looked at her with brooding intensity.

She looked at him for several seconds, a delicate blush slowly colouring her cheeks. 'We have to tell Chris about our plans yet,' she pointed out, moving away.

Reece let her go, stunned by this reminder of his son. Chris! He had completely forgotten, in his own need for Diana, that Chris would have to be told. What the hell was his son going to think of his announcement that he intended marrying the woman he had so disapproved of for him five weeks ago, the woman Chris had thought himself in love with until a short time ago? One thing was for certain: Chris wasn't going to like it!

Damn whether Chris liked it or not, was Reece's next thought. It was his life, damn it, and he would do what he damn well liked with it, including marrying someone his son was sure to think wasn't right for him either!

Diana could see that Reece had been momentarily nonplussed at the thought of telling Chris the two of them were planning to get married, and also saw, barely seconds later, that arrogance that was such an integral part of Reece take over. And she knew that at that moment Reece didn't *care* how Chris felt about the two of them as a couple.

This possible antagonism between father and son had been something she had thought might happen when she had first decided it was time the Falcon family were shaken out of their smug complacency, for them to know the same earth-shattering despair that she had known at the age of nine. But as she got to know Chris, to realise how the break-up of his parents' marriage had affected him—also at the age of nine, coincidentally—she had côme to realise that Chris was as blameless in all this as she had been. And now she had fallen in love with Reece too. Much as she loved her father, she was a dismal failure when it actually came to any sort of revenge for his death!

And Chris, she knew, was going to be totally confused at the announcement Reece intended making to him!

Although, thinking back to those speculative looks Chris had given them when they had left the party together earlier this evening, she didn't think he would be altogether surprised at there being some sort of relationship between the two of them. But marriage? Diana was sure that thought had never even crossed his mind. He would be horrified at the thought of having her as his *stepmother*!

'I'll tell him,' Reece bit out determinedly. 'Nothing is going to stand in the way of our getting married, Diana,' he added firmly.

She could see that it wasn't. And she had what she wanted now, what she had schemed for since first being introduced to Chris all those weeks ago. And it was a hollow victory, totally meaningless, because on the day she became Reece's wife *she* would lose everything that now mattered to her—Reece himself...

And no amount of persuasion on her part could get him to change his mind about the speed with which he wanted them to be married. From the moment she had agreed to marry him she found herself on the receiving end of his single-minded determination. Not that she had ever doubted that determination; it was just that marrying her was now the object of it, and he swept everything out of his path, every objection she could think of to such a hasty wedding—including the suggestion she made that people would think she was pregnant, something he grimly assured her they would know wasn't true when no baby put in an appearance!—as if it were of no consequence at all. One of the first things he did the next day, after whisking her out first thing in the morning to buy her a diamond engagement ring that sparkled so brightly it threatened to dazzle her every time she looked at it, was to invite Chris over to dinner at his apartment that evening. And Diana didn't doubt it was so that he could tell Chris about their wedding plans in private!

Reece's apartment itself was an eye-opener for Diana. She was used to staying in first-class hotels all over the world, and accepted their opulence as part of her job, but when it came to her own home she opted for comfort rather than elegance or style, and Reece's London apartment home was more lavish than any hotel suite she had ever stayed in, all chrome and glass furniture and leather seating, the walls adorned with original paintings by artists she usually had to go to a gallery to see! And he had told her in passing that he had similar homes to this one in New York, Hong Kong, and a villa in the Bahamas!

He had made no mention of Chalford...

But Diana knew he still owned the house, that it stood cared for but empty in its rural Kent setting. She had been back only once to look at it since she'd reached adulthood, had spoken briefly to the gardener there, who had told her it was owned by a chap in London called Reece Falcon, but he never used it.

The memories that seeing the house again had evoked had discouraged her from ever repeating the visit...

But even living in that grandeur herself until she was nine hadn't prepared her for Reece's style of living, and she found herself constantly on the move from one painting to another as she realised exactly what it was and who it was by. It was more than a little unnerving. And her efforts to persuade herself that the paintings and other expensive trappings of Reece's life didn't matter, because of the way he had acquired them, no longer worked, because her love for him made her doubt her own convictions that he was really as selfishly manipulative as she had believed all these years. She knew he *had* to be, because of what had happened to her father, but, at the same time, how could she love the monster she had blown Reece up in her mind to be since she was nine years old . . . ?

'It's selfish, I know,' Reece murmured softly as he came up behind her with the drinks he had just poured for them both. 'I keep all the beautiful things I own from the covetous gaze of the general public.' His mouth twisted.

Diana had turned slowly, from the painting of a young child in a field of wild daffodils, to look at him. 'Does that include women?' she challenged softly, having missed none of his tight-lipped frustration yesterday when she had told him she intended carrying on with her career after they were married. She didn't doubt, feeling as he did now, that he would be quite happy to lock her up in one of his luxury homes and throw away the key! After the fiasco any wedding between them promised to be he might still feel that way, but she doubted he would want to be locked in there with her!

Reece scowled his irritation at her astuteness, handing her the glass of orange juice she had asked for, as he thought quickly how best to answer her without causing an argument. He was still far from sure of her, despite having his engagement ring on her finger, and Diana was an intelligent woman—she would see through any prevarication on his part in answer to her question.

'I travel all over the world on business,' he began slowly. 'The last thing I want is you jetting off to New York while I'm flying to Hong Kong!'

She gave a faint smile. 'But just think of the reunions, Reece,' she gently mocked.

He had thought of little else *but* making love to this woman almost since the first moment he had looked at her, but now that he knew of her innocence he was determined to wait—no matter how much it physically pained him to do so!—until after they were married. With Diana he wanted everything to be perfect, everything they did together to be the first time for them.

'I have,' he acknowledged gruffly. 'And they wouldn't be enough for me.' He shook his head. 'Diana, I want you with me——' The slender length of her fingers against his lips silenced him, and he looked at her with impatient eyes.

'I happen to like my career, Reece,' she told him firmly. 'Enjoy it. Worked hard to get where I am today. It simply wouldn't be enough for me to sit about waiting in one luxurious hotel after another waiting for you to spare me a few minutes of your precious time between business meetings——'

'It wouldn't be like that!' he protested.

'Oh, yes,' she nodded with gentle assurance, her golden hair falling forward over her bare shoulders and down over her breasts in the dark green strapless gown she wore that clung revealingly to the slender curves of her body to just above her knee. 'It would be exactly like that.'

'No, damn it, it wouldn't't!' He took the glass out of her hand and put both drinks down on the coffee-table beside them. 'I wouldn't let it. I want to be with *you*, Diana, not stuck in some boardroom or office somewhere—— Don't laugh at me, damn you!' He scowled darkly as she chuckled softly, shaking her head indulgently.

She still smiled at him. 'Are we having our first engaged-couple argument, Reece?' she taunted softly.

Good God, so they were! And he knew exactly why. It might be part of Diana's attraction for him that she was her own person, completely independent in everything she did and said—and yet it was also damned frustrating!

He felt himself smile back at her ruefully. 'The first of many, no doubt!' he grimaced self-derisively.

She sobered suddenly, her eyes shadowed to almost as dark a green as her dress now. 'I don't like arguments, Reece,' she told him gruffly.

'But think of the making up, Diana,' he encouraged as his head slowly lowered to hers. 'Just thinking about it arouses me!'

Just thinking about it aroused her too—but it also threw her into a complete panic! She didn't have a will of her own once Reece took her in his arms. As she didn't now!

His lips moved sensually against hers, the tip of his tongue erotically outlining the softness of her mouth, flicking across the evenness of her teeth, promising much but remaining tantalising elusive.

With a low groan of capitulation Diana relaxed completely against him, her arms moving up about his neck to pull his head to her, increasing the pressure of his lips, the hardness of his body moulded against hers now.

'When no one answered the doorbell I decided to let myself in with my key,' drawled a rueful but familiar voice. 'Sorry if I'm interrupting something,' Chris added drily. 'But I thought it was tonight I was invited to dinner—— My God...Diana!' he gasped dazedly as she sprang hastily away from his father and he realised just who Reece had been kissing. 'I thought—I didn't know—— Diana...?' He gave her a pained frown of disbelief before turning to his father. 'Dad?' he snapped as indignation began to take the place of surprise.

He was demanding an explanation, from one of them, and Diana couldn't exactly blame him for feeling the way he did at finding her here with Reece. She hadn't realised he had a key to his father's apartment, although Chris had told her he'd lived here with his father until just over a year ago, so it wasn't surprising he still had the key. If only they had heard him ring the doorbell! But it was too late for 'if onlys' now; Chris had to realise there was something between his father and her now, and he had found out the worst possible way.

But Reece looked unshaken by Chris's unexpected appearance in this way, his arm moving comfortingly about her bare shoulders as he moved to stand beside her in a gesture that looked protective. 'Chris, I would like you to meet——'

'I know who she is, for God's sake!' Chris scowled darkly.

'—my fiancée,' Reece finished smoothly, as if there had been no interruption, his silver gaze challenging on his son's stunned face. 'Your future stepmother.'

Diana felt sorry for Chris at that moment. His anger had initially been replaced by confusion at the announcement, and now he looked dismayed. And she couldn't blame him for feeling that way, when he had thought himself in love with her until a short time ago. She wished she could reassure him, tell him that she would never have that place in his life, but she was trying so hard herself not to think what would happen on her wedding day when Reece found he was marrying Divinia Lambeth!

She looked at Chris with knowing sympathy. 'Chris, I——'

'Get used to the idea, Chris,' his father rasped harshly. 'The wedding is to be next month.'

That was news to her! As far as she was aware they hadn't decided on a wedding date yet. But *Reece* had, she realised as she looked at him with widely questioning eyes, frowning as it sank in that he had deliberately chosen this way to make the announcement, so putting her in a position where she couldn't deny it without Chris becoming aware of some disharmony between them concerning their wedding date. She should have guessed that Reece had accepted it too calmly when she had told him the wedding couldn't take place until her work commitments slackened off. Now that she thought about it, he had never said that he did accept it!

Chris looked taken aback at the speed with which things were happening too. 'I didn't even know the two of you—— Why?' He frowned suspiciously.

She felt Reece tense beside her, knowing he was furiously angry at the question and the way it had been put so pointedly. She gave him a knowing look; this was exactly what she had told him would happen if they married so quickly.

'Because I want Diana as my wife,' he told Chris icily. 'As soon as possible. I would marry her tomorrow if it could be arranged,' he announced arrogantly, challenge in every line of his tautly held body.

Chris had recovered slightly from his shock now, and there was a sneer to his lips as he met that challenge. 'I'm surprised it isn't, if that's what you've decided you *want*! My God——' He shook his head disgustedly. 'No wonder you were so determined *I* wasn't going to marry her; you had seen her by that time and decided you wanted Divine for yourself!'

'Her name is Diana,' Reece told him through gritted teeth at this childish act of defiance when only minutes ago Chris had been calling her Diana quite naturally. 'Or Mother, if you would prefer it,' Reece added provokingly, obviously furious at Chris's attitude.

The younger man's face became flushed with anger. 'You have got to be joking!' he scorned. 'I already have a mother, and she's thirty-eight years old. Obviously your taste runs to child-brides nowadays!' He was breathing hard in his agitation.

Diana watched the two of them as if from a great distance away. This was what she had wanted, wished for when she first met Chris: son against father, father against son, to be the instrument that destroyed each and every layer of Reece's oh, so comfortable life when he didn't hesitate to destroy others. And it was awful. Horrible. She had meant it when she told Reece she hated arguments; she hadn't been able to stand the sound of them since the day her father died.

Reece was the one in control again today, talking with that quiet stillness that could be so dangerous. 'You're the one who is behaving childishly,' he told Chris now. 'You——'

'Stop this!' she cried out—as she had so wanted to do that day in her father's study. She had always re-

gretted that she hadn't. Maybe if her father had
known she was there, that she loved him, her love
would somehow have helped him through that difficult time instead of him feeling as if he had nothing
left in the world to live for... She would never know
the answer to that question now. But what she did
know was that she couldn't stand by and listen to these
two men, who loved each other deeply, at each other's throats because of her. If nothing else, she was
going to emerge from all of this a more loving person—even if her love for Reece would ultimately destroy everything she now wanted for herself. 'Stop it,
both of you,' she choked, very pale, her eyes wide with
distress.

'Oh, hell!' Chris groaned as he saw how white she
was. 'Divine—Diana,' he amended tautly at another
fierce scowl from his father, 'I'm just—I can't believe
this is happening.' He shook his head dazedly, looking at her with pained eyes.

He had the look of puppy she had just kicked,
Diana realised emotionally.

Reece's arm tightened instinctively about her
shoulders, although his hold was still somehow gently
protective. 'We have nothing to reproach ourselves
for, Chris,' he told his son huskily. 'Nothing at all. Do
I make myself clear?' he said grimly.

Very, Diana realised ruefully, as Chris looked at
them both disbelievingly. Oh, she had told Chris from
the beginning of their friendship her views on physical relationships, and it had been something he accepted from her. But he couldn't hide his surprise at
the way his father had obviously accepted those views
too. But Reece's meaning had been clear enough...

'Yes.' Chris swallowed hard. 'I—well, I don't know what to say.' He gave an awkward shrug.

Diana felt Reece relax slightly at her side as they both sensed that the worst of the trauma had passed, that, although Chris might not be too sure he actually liked the idea of their relationship, at the same time he realised there was absolutely nothing he could do to put a stop to it, that he would have to accept it with good grace, if nothing else. Poor Chris—much as he tried, he still looked totally bewildered by the unex-pectedness of their engagement!

'"Welcome to the family" might be nice,' Reece drawled lightly. 'And then "What's for dinner?" would be appropriate.'

As he stood to one side watching intently as Chris kissed Diana on the cheek, Reece heaved an inward sigh of relief that the moment of danger was now over; he had never come so close to being completely alien-ated from his son as he had a few minutes ago. And he knew without a shadow of doubt that, no matter how painful the decision might have been, if it had come to a straight choice between his son and the woman he loved he would have chosen Diana. Not without re-gret—that was something else entirely. But he cer-tainly would have chosen Diana...

He wasn't about to win too many victories with her, though; he had known that by her skittishness earlier today over the ring he had wanted to buy her—some-thing they had compromised on in the end, the dia-mond ring not as large as the one he had wanted to buy her, but not the little one she wanted either. Compromise. Until he met Diana the word had never entered his vocabulary. The sooner he got his wedding-band on her finger beside the diamond, the more comfortable he would feel; until then he wasn't a hundred per cent certain she might not change her mind and decide not to marry him after all!

The irony of the situation struck him suddenly, and he began to smile. For years he had been avoiding matrimony with women who made no secret of the fact they wouldn't be averse to becoming the next Mrs Reece Falcon, and now the woman he *wanted* to marry was as elusive as he had been. Perhaps it was no more than he deserved, but he couldn't exactly say he liked this constant feeling of uncertainty.

And knowing Diana, as he had come to, she wasn't going to be any less determined herself even once they were married. His frown returned as he thought of her stubbornness over her career.

He would have to deal with that later. One thing at a time; he had to get his wedding-ring on her finger first!

Over the next few days Diana learnt that Reece wasn't about to be talked out of a date next month for their wedding. And once the newspapers got hold of the story of their engagement—she was almost sure it was Reece himself who had given it to them as a way of achieving his objective!—the whole thing was taken out of her control anyway.

The announcement of their engagement, of the wedding next month, was big news. Charles telephoned immediately he heard and offered her the Paris wedding gown to marry Reece in, an offer Reece was only too pleased to take him up on, telling Diana arrogantly that he couldn't allow anyone else to wear that wedding gown—not even Madeleine!—when it had been seeing her in that dress that he had first known he wanted her. Diana had never imagined when she modelled the wedding gown that she would be the bride to wear it. It almost made her cry to think of such a beautiful dress being worn on what would, ultimately, be an unhappy occasion...

She and Reece were followed everywhere they went in the days that followed the announcement, constantly photographed, articles about their movements and wedding plans emblazoned across all the more gossipy newspapers. It might almost have been a royal wedding—the queen of modelling, and the king of enterprise was how one newspaper described them. It was rubbish, of course, but it sold newspapers, Diana realised cynically.

And once the initial razzmatazz had passed there came the speculation of their future life together, of where they would live after the wedding—although Diana hadn't known what they thought was wrong with Reece's apartment!—and, finally, how many little 'princes and princesses' they would have to inherit that vast wealth.

This latter speculation startled Diana to start with, and then she felt only disgust. It was all so utterly ridiculous anyway, when Reece already had an heir in Chris. But the newspapers seemed determined to speculate, much to Reece's displeasure. 'They'll be picking out names for us next!' Diana pushed one of the newspapers away in disgust, looking across at Reece as the two of them relaxed together in the sitting-room of her flat after eating the meal they had enjoyed preparing together.

It all looked so cosy, she realised with regret; she was finding these increasing day-to-day intimacies between them more than a little disturbing, and knew that she was actually beginning to anticipate their evenings together, to enjoy the time they spent alone together.

And she knew without a doubt that it would all come to an end the moment Reece knew who she really was. Her face became shadowed as she thought of that time, a time that would happen all too quickly if Reece had his way—as he seemed determined he would!—and they were married within the next few weeks. She knew now she could no longer wait until the wedding, that she couldn't do that to him so publicly, that she would have to tell him before it came to that.

She felt the inner pain as she thought of how lonely her life was going to seem without him now. For years it hadn't bothered her that she lived alone; in fact she had preferred it. But now, she acknowledged, she knew that was because she had never realised before how much loving someone could fill your life. Or how much being without that person could empty it again...

'Diana, you have to know, I don't want any more children!'

The harshness of Reece's statement broke into the misery of the emotional dilemma she had made for herself by falling in love with this man.

She frowned at him now, at the grimness of his expression. 'Reece...?'

He stood up abruptly, hands thrust into his trouser pockets. 'I'm thirty-nine years old, Diana, forty in a few months' time; that's too old to be a father again!'

It was because she had known there was no point in even thinking about the two of them having children that the speculation in the newspapers had seemed so ridiculous. But as she looked up at Reece's pale face she knew he had given the subject serious thought...

'I've always believed it was the mother's age that was the important one,' she said slowly.

'My life wasn't geared for having children the first time around,' Reece rasped, eyes narrowed. 'It's even less so now!'

Diana shook her head at his vehemence. 'Shouldn't this be something we sit down and decide together?' She didn't even know why she was being so persistent—there would be no children between them anyway, so the conversation was utterly pointless. But at the same time this seemed very important.

Reece was still stony-faced. 'Is it going to be relevent to whether or not you marry me?'

'No.' She shook her head dazedly. 'But——'

'No children, Diana,' he told her harshly. 'It isn't true that they enrich a marriage,' he added less forcibly as he saw how stunned she was by his determination. 'Children cause more strain between a married couple than anything else.'

She frowned up at him. 'Is that what happened between you and Cathy?'

He scowled at the mention of his first wife. 'I don't want to discuss her with you—— Don't look like that,' he groaned at the hurt puzzlement in her face, moving to sit on the floor beside her. 'I just don't happen to think discussing what went wrong in my first marriage is going to help the two of us now, that's all,' he told her cajolingly, one lean hand moving up to caress the creamy softness of her cheek. 'It just opens up old wounds, past bitterness.'

Diana didn't happen to agree with him; she thought that talking about what had happened in the past might possibly help not to make the same mistakes again—as she had been doing, by trying to hurt Reece in the way she had! She should have known it was stupid, irrational. That old saying Nanny used to recite to her as a child had never been more true—'two wrongs don't make a right'. What they made, what *she* had made, for both of them, was just future misery on top of the past.

God, there had to be some way she could make things right between herself and Reece after all. A way, loving Reece as she did, that she could marry him after all. There *had* to be!

But when she opened the door to her flat the next morning and saw who her visitor was, she knew there wasn't...

CHAPTER NINE

'WELL, are you going to keep me standing on the doorstep all day?' Janette drawled mockingly. 'Or are you going to invite me inside?'

Diana just stared at her, too stunned to speak, to move. She hadn't seen Janette for years, five to be exact. What was she doing here now? Why now? It couldn't just be coincidence, could it . . .?

'Really, Divinia,' her stepmother said scathingly as she made no reply to her opening sarcasm. 'I would have thought that expensive school you attended would have taught you better manners than this!' She brushed past Diana and into the flat, leaving a trail of expensive perfume in her wake as she paused to look curiously in the rooms she passed on the way to the sitting-room, wrinkling her nose with delicate distaste as she entered this room and saw the lack of furniture, but large bean-bags instead and scatter-rugs on the floor. 'Everyone to their own taste, I suppose,' she said with dismissive scorn as she turned fully to look back at Diana.

Diana had followed more slowly, stunned at seeing the other woman again after all this time. The years had been kinder to Janette than she perhaps deserved, and, at thirty-seven, she was still undoubtedly a beautiful woman: small and delicately built, with an air of fragility that was wholly deceptive—Janette had a band of steel running through her emotions that didn't become apparent until she was opposed, and *then* she wasn't in the least fragile!—her blonde hair a silken bob to her shoulders, her eyes a deep blue, any ageing of her face hidden by expertly applied make-up.

Diana—Divinia, as she had still been then—had been sixteen years old the last time the two of them had met, her long coltish limbs and gawky body more of an enemy to her then than an asset, having a total lack of self-assurance because of her height and too-slender curves. But if Janette had changed little over the last five years Diana knew that *she* had changed a great deal, and now that she had had time to gather her scattered wits together she faced the older woman across the room with cool assurance.

Janette looked her up and down derisively, duly noting the casual elegance with which Diana wore the denims and loose-fitting T-shirt. 'So the ugly duckling turned into a swan!' she taunted.

She had never been an 'ugly duckling', merely a slow developer, and both women knew it; it was just Janette's way of trying to put her at a disadvantage. But she wasn't about to succeed, the intervening years having given Diana a calm confidence as well as maturing her body. And, for all her derision, she knew just how hard Janette had to work at her own supposedly natural blonde beauty.

She eyed the older woman coldly. 'What do you want, Janette?'

'A cup of coffee might be nice, thank you.' Janette sat down on the one piece of furniture in the room that was suitable—a high-backed wing-chair, crossing one silky leg over the other, her skin looking deeply tanned against the fitted white dress she wore, a fact Diana was sure she was well aware of. 'I only stopped off at my hotel long enough to drop off my luggage,' she shrugged.

Diana didn't move. 'That wasn't what I meant, and you know it.' She sighed at the pointlessness of this pretence of any politeness between them.

Blue eyes narrowed coldly. 'Surely a cup of coffee is the least you can give me?' Janette rasped harshly.

Diana met her gaze steadily. 'I don't owe you anything. Not even a cup of coffee,' she added pointedly.

Fury suddenly glittered in those hard blue eyes. 'You owe me a damn sight more than——' Janette broke off abruptly, drawing in a deep breath as she regained control. 'The coffee on planes is always awful,' she spoke in that slightly bored drawl now that was so typical of her. 'And I remember that making coffee was one of the few things you were good at.'

Considering that on those few brief weeks during the school holidays when she had been invited to join Janette and Marco at their villa the two of them had treated her as nothing more than a glorified maid, Janette should be more than aware of how good her coffee was—Cinderella hadn't even come into it! Although Janette wasn't exactly the wicked stepmother of the fairy-story, just an incredibly selfish woman.

'Anyway,' Janette added softly, 'we have such a lot to talk about—don't you agree?'

No, Janette's presence here now wasn't a coincidence... Obviously the other woman had seen the announcement of her engagement to Reece, and the publicity that had followed, in the newspapers. And the last thing Janette lacked, with her inborn deviousness, was intelligence!

Nevertheless, Diana deliberately kept her gaze steady with the older woman's. 'I can't think of a single thing, to be honest,' she dismissed drily, deliberately being obtuse. 'But as I haven't had coffee myself yet this morning I suppose I could make us a pot.'

'So gracious,' Janette muttered.

Diana gave her a bright, meaningless smile before leaving the room to go to the kitchen, her breath leaving her body in a shaky sigh once she reached the relative sanctuary of the other room, where she took a few minutes' respite to steady her nerves before even thinking about making the coffee.

It was obvious that Janette knew of her relationship with Reece, but what Diana was unsure of was what she had hoped to achieve by coming here. Because Janette never did anything without a specific purpose in mind.

Diana gave a start of surprise as Puddle brushed against her leg, so lost had she been in her worried thoughts. And as she looked down at the cat she was almost sure she saw sympathy for her plight in the intelligent lime-green eyes.

'A ghost from my past, Puddle,' she told him softly, bending down to stroke one silky ear distractedly before automatically making the coffee, moving like an automaton now, her thoughts deeply inward.

Seeing Janette again after all this time *was* a little like being confronted with a ghost from her past. And until a very short time ago she had been living in that past herself, with the painful memories it evoked, and now she was only left with the powerful love she felt for Reece—and that terrible fear she had of losing him, a fear she knew would all too soon be a reality. Whatever hopes she had gone to bed with the previous night about the possibility of being able to marry Reece after all, without telling him about her father, were now dashed with Janette's arrival here. If Janette once realised she was trying to keep that information from Reece, then she knew from experience that the other woman would take great pleasure in telling him the truth herself. In fact, Diana couldn't think of any other reason for Janette's being here...!

'Nemesis might be a better description of her, Puddle,' she told the cat heavily as she prepared the coffee-tray.

'Talking to a cat now?' drawled a taunting voice from the doorway, and Diana looked up sharply to find Janette standing there looking at her with mockingly raised brows. 'I heard you talking to someone,' she explained her presence there with a dismissive shrug. 'I thought perhaps you might have another visitor. One you didn't want me to meet,' she added challengingly.

Reece. She meant Reece. Because if Reece saw Janette here he was sure to question their friendship. And once he realised they weren't friends at all... Reece was far too intelligent not to eventually add two and two together and come up with the correct answer of four. If Janette didn't tell him the truth first, that was! Although there was no danger of the two of them meeting this morning; Reece was working today, and he had known she was relaxing this morning before going to a photographic session this afternoon.

'But then,' Janette added scornfully, 'you always were rather over-sentimental when it came to animals, weren't you?'

They both knew the other woman was referring to Diana's pony Honey now, a gift from her father on her seventh birthday, sold along with everything else after her father's death to help pay the debts. At the time Divinia had been too numbed to really notice his going, but months later she had broken her heart over it.

'The coffee is ready.' Diana pointedly picked up the laden tray in preparation for going into the other room with it.

Janette stepped tauntingly to one side to let her pass, the thin heels of her shoes tapping on the wooden floor as she followed Diana down the hallway. 'Such an— interesting choice of décor,' she drawled as she sat down once again, watching with narrowed eyes as Diana poured the coffee.

She looked across at the other woman from her kneeling position on the floor. 'You didn't come here to criticise my flat.' She sighed her impatience with the delay.

'Didn't I?' Janette sipped the freshly brewed coffee appreciatively. 'No, perhaps not,' she acknowledged softly. 'Does Reece know you're only marrying him out of a sense of revenge?'

Diana felt as if all the breath had been knocked from her body at the directness of this attack, the colour draining from her cheeks. She had been expecting this, should have been ready for it, and yet she now felt completely breathless.

Janette watched her with slightly raised brows, completely unruffled by the accusation she had just calmly made. 'I'm right, aren't I?' she said knowingly. 'Reece has no idea that the model Divine, his beautiful Diana, is actually Divinia Lambeth, does he?' she taunted, gaining in confidence all the time as she saw the truth of her words in Diana's ashen face.

Diana swallowed hard. 'My relationship with Reece is none of your business——'

'Oh, but it is,' Janette smiled confidently. 'You see, I'm going through a rather messy divorce at the moment Oh, yes, I'm divorcing Marco.' Her mouth twisted bitterly. 'Have decided after all these years that I really can't take any more of his behaviour. Unfortunately, for me, he made me sign one of those nasty little pre-marital agreements that means I get a mere pittance in allowance if there should be a divorce——'

'Then don't divorce him,' Diana said without sympathy. But she had to admit to being more than a little surprised Janette should be taking such a step, mainly because she couldn't imagine Janette taking such exception to anything that Marco did that she would feel the need to divorce him. As far as she was aware, Janette had been blatantly ignoring everything her faithless husband did since she first married him.

Hard blue eyes narrowed icily at the dismissive statement. 'It isn't as simple as that——'

'Things never were where Marco was concerned,' Diana said with remembered disgust.

'You aren't going to start on about that again, are you?' Janette sighed her impatient irritation.

Her eyes flashed deeply green at the bored dismissal. 'You *knew* your husband had tried to rape me, a sixteen-year-old innocent——'

'Oh, don't talk such rot, Divinia,' Janette snapped coldly, her face twisted into an ugly mask. 'Marco has never had any reason to rape any woman, no matter what her age; they've always been waiting in line to give it away!' she added with distaste for her husband's appetites.

'And what about the ones who didn't *want* to give it away?' Diana demanded incredulously. The memory of that day with Marco was almost as traumatic as her father's death. And she had never been able to understand the other woman's attitude then—or since!—when she had run to her crying hysterically, after Marco had attacked her next to their pool.

Janette had been resting in her room that afternoon with one of her 'headaches'—recovering from a hangover from the night before might have described it more accurately!—and Divinia, lounging by the pool after a brief swim, had been taken completely by surprise when Marco began to compliment her more intimately than ever before on her budding body.

Oh, the Italian could be charming, and, like a lot of Latin men, a little flirtatious, and he had teased her since her arrival the week before about how quickly she was growing up.

But this time it hadn't been teasing or flirtatious, and it had all too soon become ugly and degrading, with Divinia only just managing to push him away and escape inside the villa, her mouth swollen from the force of his lips on hers.

Janette hadn't believed her when she had run to tell her what had happened. Or, at least, she had said she didn't, brushing the whole incident away as the exaggerated result of a too-active imagination combined with a crush on an older man.

The *last* thing Diana had ever felt was attracted to Marco. In fact, for the remainder of that holiday she had stayed in her bedroom, with the door locked, where she didn't have to see him. And she had never again accepted any of Janette and Marco's invitations to stay with them, feeling as betrayed by Janette's lack of belief in her as she was by Marco's actions.

'I didn't come here to discuss the past, Divinia,' Janette told her chidingly now. 'The thing is, because of the divorce, I'm a little short of cash right now, and I'm sure, until you have Reece's wedding-ring firmly on your finger, that you would rather he——'

'No!' Diana cut in harshly, her eyes dark with pain. 'What you're talking about is blackmail, Janette, and I——'

'What an ugly word.' Janette winced with exaggerated pain.

'Blackmail *is* an ugly word.' She looked at the other woman disgustedly. 'It's an ugly word to describe an ugly deed.'

'All I'm asking is that you help me out with a little money until I can sort things out with Marco.' Janette pouted her irritation. 'You don't——' She broke off as the doorbell rang. 'More visitors?' she drawled. 'Not a lover, surely, Divinia?' she taunted as Diana looked flustered at this second intrusion of the morning.

'Don't be ridiculous!' She stood up abruptly; whoever it was at the door, she had to get rid of them, and quickly. The sooner she settled this situation with Janette, the better. Much as she hated the thought of what the other woman was suggesting, at the same time it gave her a small glimmer of hope that perhaps she could make things right between herself and Reece after all!

Janette nodded, smiling slightly. 'Knowing Reece as I do, that would be just a little too dangerous, darling. I should imagine he would make a very jealous fiancé.'

'As opposed to a lover?' Diana snapped, bright spots of colour in her otherwise pale cheeks.

Janette's smile became rueful. 'That could be another one of those little things we discuss—once you've got rid of your visitor, of course.' She frowned her irritation as the doorbell rang intrusively a second time. 'Persistent little devil, whoever it is!' She brushed away an imaginary speck from her white dress before looking up at Diana expectantly.

Diana turned and fled the room, shaking badly as she went out into the hallway. She couldn't believe this was happening to her. And it was all her own fault. If she had never gone near Reece . . .!

And she wasn't fooled for a moment by Janette's explanation of her divorce now that she had had even a short time to think about it; she knew there had to be more to that than Janette was telling her.

But, whatever the real reasons for Janette's divorce from Marco, it had pushed Janette into coming here to ask for money. Blackmail, Diana had called it, and blackmail it was!

She felt herself sway dizzily as she opened the door and found Reece standing there! She should have known who the 'persistent little devil' was, should have guessed. Instead she felt as if she had received yet another blow to her solar plexus.

'Diana!' he groaned softly, making no effort to take her in his arms. 'I had to come and see you.' He was very pale, a nerve pulsing in his cheek. 'I owe you some sort of explanation for last night.'

Last night? She stared at him, dumbfounded; what had happened last night?

He had spent a long, restless night going over and over in his mind the dilemma he had put himself in, had dressed and gone to the office this morning knowing it was a waste of time—that he had to see Diana. He knew now, after hours of wrestling with his conscience, that he couldn't even think of marrying her without telling her the truth about himself. And he wasn't looking forward to it.

He had gone through a whole gamut of emotions and uncertainties through those long hours of sleeplessness during the night. Guilt. Pain. Tenderness. Love. But most of all he had known fear, as he had never experienced it before. He was terrified of losing Diana.

Diana, on closer inspection, didn't look any better than he did. She was very pale, and there was a haunted look in her eyes.

Reece felt himself tense when Diana moved away from him as he would have taken her in his arms. Had she already guessed the truth? Did she know? Or had she just realised, as she lay in her own lonely bed, that she couldn't accept what he had said to her? Oh, God, they had to talk!

'I don't know what you mean, Reece.' She shook her head in confusion, looking incredibly young and oh, so vulnerable at that moment. 'And now isn't really a good time to talk about it.'

He knew she had an assignment this afternoon, but he also knew there was never going to be a 'good' time to talk about this, and he was tensed up to do it now. 'It has to be now, Diana,' he told her softly—before he lost his nerve and just grabbed at her with both hands and took the consequences for deceiving her after they were married!

'No!' She held her hand up in apology as she realised how sharply she had spoken. 'You don't understand, Reece,' she added shakily. 'It isn't convenient just now. I—have a visitor.'

His frowned deepened, and he looked at her more intently. She had been behaving oddly ever since she'd opened the door and saw him standing there, now that he thought about it, but at the time he had put that down to the fact that she must be upset about last night too. But he realised now that she was standing almost defensively in the doorway, that she obviously didn't want to invite him inside.

Obviously she didn't want him to see whoever it was she had in there! Who the hell could it be that she was behaving so defensively?

Jealousy ripped through him the way he imagined the burning sensation of a knife being thrust into his chest would feel, and he pushed past her effortlessly to take determined steps in the direction of the sitting-room. If it was Chris she had in there——!

Because there was something else he had realised as he'd lain awake last night: Diana might have agreed to marry him, might wear his ring on her finger, but not once had she ever told him she loved him...! She had to love him; why else would she have agreed to marry him? But even so——

'Reece!' She hurried after him now, clutching at his arm. 'Reece, listen to me!' she cried pleadingly before he could open the door to the sitting-room. 'It isn't what you think!'

He was trying not to 'think' at all, and as he threw open the door to find it was a woman who stood there and not the man he had been expecting he felt totally confused. Except... It might be twelve years since he'd last seen this woman, but she hadn't changed much, was still beautifully alluring to look at—and mercenary as hell! Janette Lambeth. No, that wasn't her name now, because she had remarried not long after Howard's death—some Italian if he remembered correctly. What the hell did it matter who this woman had married, or what she had done in the years since he had last seen her? What he wanted to know was what was she doing *here*, in Diana's home? Surely the two of them weren't friends? He wouldn't have said Janette was Diana's type of person at all. But then, how well did he really know the woman he was going to marry...?

She wanted to die. Wanted the ground to open up and swallow her down into it, leaving not a trace of her presence here. And then these two people who were left, both of them looking wary now, could thrash out the details of her involvement with Reece between them.

And they would both be wrong. Because, whatever her initial motivation in setting out to captivate Reece, she now loved him more than life itself. And after today she knew she was going to have to live without him . . .

'Diana?' he questioned harshly.

Janette was looking at her too, furious as she realised her ploy to blackmail Diana was no longer going to work. The hardness of her gaze promised retribution for that as she glared at Diana.

And then the cold fury was replaced by a lightly charming smile as she turned to Reece. 'Don't be so distant, Reece,' she all but purred. 'We're old— friends, remember?' She looked at him with warm knowing eyes.

Diana felt sick at the thought of the two of them together. 'Yes, Reece,' she choked. 'Don't you remember?'

The tender lover she had known since he'd asked her to marry him had now gone, and in his place was the steely eyed Reece Falcon she had met in Paris all those weeks ago, a man who didn't suffer fools gladly—and who wouldn't suffer being deceived at all! That sick feeling in the pit of Diana's stomach intensified.

'Janette.' He nodded abrupt acknowledgement in her direction, not by word or deed confirming that he 'remembered' anything! But, at the same time, the fact that he acknowledged the other woman at all was indication that he remembered her only too well! 'I wasn't aware that the two of you knew each other?' His eyes were narrowed to steely slits.

'Oh, yes.' Janette was back in command of her emotions now, well aware that she had lost out in the nasty game she had intended playing with Diana, but also realising that she hadn't lost completely, that she could still enjoy herself—at Diana's expense! 'I don't believe you met Divinia all those years ago, did you?' she drawled conversationally. 'But she's certainly grown into a beauty, hasn't she?' She arched blonde brows.

'Divinia...?' Reece frowned. 'But I—you——' He faltered as the truth obviously began to dawn on him.

Diana, watching him, wanted to cry out once again that it wasn't what he thought it was, wanted to *scream* the denial at him. But the saddest part of all this, she acknowledged, for both Reece and herself—her identity having at last been realised, she could see by his stunned expression—was that in the beginning she had only wanted to get to know him so that she could make him suffer as her father had, as she had in the years that followed. But it wasn't true now. God, it wasn't true now...!

Divinia Lambeth...

For a moment Reece was so dazed—gobsmacked, as he had once described his reaction to Diana!—by the realisation that this was who Diana Lamb *really* was that he couldn't think at all!

And then it all came back to him with sickening clarity: that pointless meeting with Howard Lambeth when he had tried to discuss the financial situation with the other man—something he had realised was completely futile in the light of the other man's state

of mind at the time, resulting in Reece's leaving before the insults got out of hand.

He had driven all the way back to London that day
inwardly cursing the other man's stupidity, only to
arrive back at his apartment to see on the evening news
that there had been some sort of shooting accident at
Lambeth's home, and that the other man had received fatal injuries. Only hours before, Reece had
tried to reason with the man, and suddenly he was
dead...!

Janette, hysterical and accusing, floundering herself
in a morass of uncertainties, had been the one to telephone him and tell him Howard's death hadn't been
an accident at all—that the other man had deliberately shot himself. And that his nine-year-old daughter had been in the room at the time...

Diana, Reece now realised, had been that nine-year-
old child who had witnessed her father shooting himself—and, as Reece well knew, had suffered months of
emotional trauma after it.

So much of the woman she was today was explained now—that elusive coolness, the distant self-
possession in one so young. Diana Lamb was a prod-
uct of that young Divinia Lambeth.

And Divinia Lambeth believed she had reason to
hate him...

Diana watched him still, knowing he was remembering, as she did, everything that had happened in her
father's study that day, and she saw the dawning
comprehension on Reece's face now, his anguish, the
pain as he realised exactly why she was in his life now.

And she knew that he suffered as he realised she hadn't ever been motivated by love for him, saw the pain of that realisation ripping him apart, tearing at his innermost emotions.

It was what she had wanted to happen so long ago in that dark nightmare before she had loved him. But now, loving him as deeply as she did, she knew as deep an agony herself. Because it was all over for them now; Reece would never believe her if she told him she loved him, had fallen in love with him in spite of herself. And who could blame him if he just thought it was another deceit on her part, another way of hurting him? He would never trust her again.

She looked at Janette, the woman her father had married and then entrusted to take care of her after his death, and saw the smile of triumph on the other woman's lips as she knew—she *knew*—how badly Diana had failed in her loyalty to her father.

And then she looked at Reece, a Reece with eyes so black with disillusionment that they were like twin coals of burning emotion.

And Diana knew she couldn't stand any more, that she had to get away. She, who had tried never to run away from anything in her life, had to go. And now.

She turned and fled, tears choking in her throat as Reece called after her, knowing that he probably wanted the pleasure of choking her himself!

The need to escape was paramount. She didn't care where she went, only knew she had to get as far away from Reece and Janette as she possibly could!

The people who crowded the street outside were just a sea of faces to her, dark, curiously intent faces as she burst on to the pavement not knowing which way to go. Several people stopped to stare openly as they obviously recognised her, and with another anguished cry she turned to run away from them too!

She didn't even see the car, didn't even feel its impact with her body; she only knew the blessed relief of the blackness that engulfed her as her head struck the ground . . .

CHAPTER TEN

THE minutes ticked by as if they were hours. So slowly, so very slowly. And as they passed with agonising slowness Reece sat in the chair beside the bed, unmoving himself, his gaze riveted on the soft rise and fall of Diana's breasts as she lay so still beneath the bedclothes, her face almost as white as the sheets themselves—or the thick bandage that swathed her head to cover the deep gash she had sustained when she first fell on to the road and was knocked unconscious.

There were no other injuries; the car—a taxi that had just picked up a fare and was moving away from the pavement—hadn't been travelling fast enough to do more than actually knock Diana off-balance.

No other injuries that showed, Reece acknowledged heavily. But inside Diana was a pain he knew would never go away: that of losing her father in the way that she had.

How she must hate him, must have hated him all these years. He hadn't known that day twelve years ago, hadn't realised just how desperate Lambeth was. If only Howard had listened to him, none of this—— But the other man had been too angry that day to be reasoned with, hadn't wanted to hear anything Reece had to say, and so in the end Reece had left him, intending to talk to Howard when he was in a more reasonable frame of mind. Reece had rebuked himself time and time again for not having realised there would never be another day for Howard, but in the end he had had to accept that he was punishing himself for something that couldn't be altered—that it was the living that counted.

Diana, for whom the nightmare was a continuous thing, hadn't been given that luxury...

He had known Lambeth had a young daughter—of course he had; but it had never occurred to him, not even for a moment, that Diana was that child. God, he could kick himself now when he remembered how casually he had dismissed from his mind that lack of information Paul had come up with on Diana's childhood, how he had been so sure it wasn't important, that it was the woman she was now that mattered. How wrong he had been! Diana's painful childhood was what had *made* her the woman she was today.

Which woman was she going to be when she woke up—the one who had agreed to marry him and then hesitated about fixing a date for the wedding, or the one who had hated him enough to engineer this whole thing so that she could make him pay for his part in her father's death?

If she woke up. The doctors had warned him there could be an 'if' involved in that. The blow to her head had knocked her unconscious, and so far, twelve hours later, she had shown no signs of coming out of it. And the longer she remained unconscious, the more afraid the doctors were that she could go into a coma without ever regaining consciousness, suffering from an

internal injury they had no control over. Reece
couldn't bear even to think about the possibility;
Diana had already suffered enough. Except...what
did she really have, in her own injured mind, at least,
to wake up for?

'No change?' Chris appeared at his side, having
been at the hospital on and off all day himself—the
doctors were not too happy about letting Reece stay in
with Diana all the time, and flatly refused to let any
other full-time visitors stay.

'No change,' Reece acknowledged heavily. And yet
his life had been changed forever by this ethereally
lovely woman who lay so still and unmoving. And, no
matter what the future held for *them*, she had to recover. She *had* to!

It was so nice floating in this world of half-light, so
peaceful, so still, nothing to—— But she could hear
the soft murmur of voices, half recognised them,
frowning as she tried to remember who—— But the
voices had gone away again now, leaving her to the
grey darkness that cocooned and carried her...

But she wasn't being left in peace now—she could
hear a voice again. Just a single voice, talking softly,
a voice that was so achingly familiar now as she remembered...remembered—Reece! It was Reece,
talking so gently. But who was he talking to?

'I'm so sorry, Diana—Divinia—— God, I don't
even know what to call you any more!' he groaned
huskily.

Her. He was talking to *her*. She was Diana—wasn't
she...? She wasn't sure. She thought she was.

She wanted to open her eyes and look at him—
maybe then she would know who she was; but her lids
felt so heavy, so very heavy.

'You have to wake up, Diana. You *have* to,' he told
her more forcefully.

Diana. She was Diana. Divinia, whatever traces of
her had been left, had disappeared when she fell in
love with this man. And she did love him, was sure
that she did, the sound of his voice waking her. But
what was he sorry for? She didn't understand.

'I have so much to tell you,' he groaned, his hand
clasping the limpness of one of hers as it lay on the bed
beside her. 'So much to explain!'

She was listening; didn't he know she was listening?

'I'm going to be here when you wake up, damn it,'
Reece rasped as she still lay so still. 'I don't care when
it is—I'm going to be the first person you see when
you open your eyes!'

She wanted to smile at his arrogance, to tell him he
was the person she wanted to see when she woke up,
but it was all too much for her, she realised, when she
tried to return the clasp of his hand and knew she had
failed, the deep heaviness of sleep claiming her once
again.

Today was the day. It could be delayed no longer.
And, whether it turned out a disaster or not, Reece
knew he couldn't stand the strain another day longer.

Diana wasn't in the bed when he entered her room,
and for a brief moment he felt panic course through
him. And then he saw her through the open french
windows, sitting in the sunshine, looking out over the

hospital gardens, her face pale in profile, the bandage completely gone from her brow now, just a small dressing in its place to cover the wound that had received half a dozen stitches.

It was almost a week since she had regained consciousness and all the doctors' fears—and his own!— concerning brain damage had been put to rest. Apart from that gash, and a king-sized headache, Diana seemed to have escaped the accident unharmed.

And since that time the two of them had been dodging the issue completely that had caused her to take flight in the first place!

It wasn't like Reece to be so cowardly, but he was very much aware that this time he was facing possibly the greatest challenge of his life, that there was still so much to lose. And he was far from sure of the outcome.

For her part, Diana seemed as reluctant to face the confrontation as he. And as the two of them were so rarely alone, Chris usually accompanying him on his visits to the hospital, or one of Diana's model friends already in the room with her, it hadn't been so difficult to avoid the subject of the past; in fact, it had been virtually impossible to bring it up!

But today it would be different; today Diana was due to go home. And Reece was the one who was going to drive her there.

She turned to look at him now, as if sensing his presence, the green gaze becoming suddenly wary as she sensed too that the time for prevaricating was at an end.

She stood up calmly, wearing the clothes she had asked one of her friends to call at the flat and collect

for her the day before: a light woollen top the same
colour as her eyes, and a floral skirt in autumn colours that reached almost to her ankles. Her hair was
newly washed, a golden cascade down her spine, that
small dressing on her brow adding to her look of vulnerability.

She had never, apart from that time when she modelled the Oxley wedding gown—and just thinking
about *that* twisted a knife inside him!—looked love-
lier to him.

She felt like a sacrificial lamb being driven to her
slaughter. Reece had been very patient this last week,
but they both knew his patience was at an end. She
was going to know that heart-wrenching pain again,
to know exactly what it was like to lose him.

And who could blame him? She had been found
out, exposed, and Reece wasn't a forgiving man. She
was prepared, if not exactly fortified, for the ordeal
that lay ahead of her.

What she wasn't prepared for was Janette waiting
outside her flat for them when they arrived there!

And, from the mutinous expression on Janette's
face as she joined them, she wasn't there through
choice either! 'I have a plane to catch in a couple of
hours,' she snapped irritably. 'So if we could just try
and keep all of this short?'

'You'll stay as long as it takes, Janette,' Reece told
her hardly as Diana let them into the flat with her key,
the flat feeling very empty, Puddle still being over with
Roger.

She wasn't altogether sure she was going to stand up
under the strain of this; the journey from the hospital, full of tension, had already tired her—and now

this. She had known she and Reece had to talk, but this promised to be so much worse than that would have been, and the pounding in her head told her she would have to sit down soon—or fall down!

'Go into the sitting-room,' Reece instructed harshly after looking at her with narrowed eyes. 'I'll make us all some coffee and bring it through——

'I don't have time for coffee,' Janette told him sharply.

He returned her gaze coldly. 'There are two other people here who do,' he told her in a voice that brooked no further argument, before going off assuredly in the direction of the kitchen.

Diana dropped down wearily on to one of the big bean-bags, closing her eyes briefly, only to find when she opened them again seconds later that Janette was looking down at her with open scorn. 'Why don't you sit down?' Diana invited dully. 'This seems to be Reece's show.'

'Arrogant bastard!' Janette muttered resentfully as she sat down on the edge of the only chair in the room. 'Marco has at last agreed to be reasonable and sit down and discuss a divorce settlement, and instead of flying back to Italy as I want to do before he changes his mind and divorces me without——'

'*Marco* is divorcing *you*?' Diana stared; this wasn't the way Janette had originally told it.

The other woman looked flustered. 'What difference does it make who divorces who?' Her face was very flushed in her agitation.

'None at all.' Diana shrugged dismissively. 'I just thought——'

'Marco has decided it's time for a newer model, all right?' Janette snapped, her mouth twisting sneeringly. 'He's found himself a cute little redhead from Texas, only twenty-three, with a very rich daddy. I should have realised his taste ran to young girls after he tried to make love to you——'

'You always said you didn't believe me about that!' Diana gasped.

'Look, I just want to get out of here.' Janette looked around her impatiently. 'I would have been at the airport now if Reece hadn't seen fit to demand my presence here instead!'

Diana didn't have time to dwell on what Janette had just admitted knowing about Marco five years ago as Reece strode back into the room.

'And you know damned well why I demanded that,' he rasped.

Janette tilted her head back defiantly. 'I don't for one minute believe you would have gone through with prosecuting me!'

Grey eyes narrowed to icy cold slits. 'Try me,' Reece invited softly.

Diana watched the exchange with puzzled eyes. She felt a little stronger now after having sat for a few minutes—but, at the same time, she didn't have the vaguest idea what these two were talking about!

Janette paled slightly beneath tanned cheeks. 'She didn't suffer——'

'Didn't she?' Reece scorned incredulously, shaking his head disgustedly. 'Maybe not by your standards, Janette,' he accepted insultingly. 'But, by all that's decent, the next eight years of her life, at least, were a nightmare for her!'

'Implying my standards aren't decent!' Janette realised heatedly, standing up now, her face twisted into an ugly mask. 'I don't have to stay here to be insulted like this——'

'No,' Reece acknowledged just as angrily. 'To quote an old cliché, "You could go *anywhere* and be insulted in exactly the same way"!' His eyes glittered dangerously. 'But don't have any doubts about it, Janette; you are going to stay right here until the truth has finally been told. And then you can go anywhere you please!' Hell and back, for all he cared, his tone implied.

Diana was still completely in the dark about the meaning of their conversation, and she could have screamed her frustration when Reece chose that moment to go back into the kitchen and pour the coffee! Janette didn't give the impression that she was prepared to enlighten her either, shooting her a venomous look before flouncing off to stare out of the large window, her back firmly turned on Diana. But she was worried; Diana could tell that by the way she fidgeted constantly.

And by the time Reece finally came in with the laden tray Diana herself was a bundle of nerves. 'Will someone please tell me what all this is about?' she demanded impatiently.

Reece arched dark brows pointedly at the resentful Janette who had now turned back to face them. 'Well?' he prompted tautly.

Her cheeks were flushed with anger. 'Why the hell do I have to be the one——? Oh, all right!' she snapped furiously as his expression took on a dangerous quality, and she turned impatiently to Diana.

'After your father's—death,' she bit out resentfully, every word obviously forced out of her, 'Reece made us an allowance—— Oh, all *right*, he made you an allowance,' she corrected as Reece's mouth thinned warningly. 'For your schooling to continue. Holidays. Things like that,' she dismissed. 'But as your legal guardian I was to administer the allowance,' she added defensively.

'And the rest,' Reece grated. 'Chalford,' he reminded tautly, his head back challengingly.

'Her birthday was only three months ago, for God's sake,' Janette snapped. 'I've had a lot of other things on my mind during that time than trying to remember exactly when Divinia reached twenty-one!'

'Your problems with your errant husband are none of my concern,' Reece dismissed with distaste for the subject. '*Diana*, however, is!'

'Divinia, Diana, what difference does it matter what I call her?' the other woman said impatiently.

'Indeed,' he acknowledged with a slow inclination of his head, his gaze steady on her. 'It's what should have been hers, which you took for yourself, that matters!'

Diana was feeling ill again. *Reece* was the reason she had been able to stay on at her boarding-school, and not because there had been enough money left over from her father's estate. But why had he done that— unless he had a guilty conscience about the way her father had died...?

'I needed the money.' Janette was too agitated herself to realise just how angry Reece was—and he was *very* angry indeed, the cold fury emanating from him. 'How else was I suppose to live?' she defended.

'Until you could find yourself a husband rich enough to continue supporting you in that extravagant lifestyle you had so come to love!' Reece accused disgustedly. 'You stole from a child, Janette,' he said incredulously. 'A child who had already suffered a shock so severe it had left her with lasting scars.'

Janette gave a harsh laugh. 'She took something of mine too, once she was old enough to realise how susceptible Marco was to a young lissom body!'

'That isn't true!' Diana gasped, at last able to contribute something to a conversation that was becoming more and more incredible by the minute. 'I was just sixteen, Reece,' she told him defensively. 'Had no idea—certainly didn't want—Marco tried to rape me!' She swallowed hard at Reece's sharply indrawn breath. 'And when I told Janette she said she didn't believe me.' She looked at the other woman accusingly now for what she had admitted to the contrary such a short time ago. How could she have done that to a young child?

'Of course I believed you,' the other woman admitted again. 'I had had to sit by for months watching as Marco's interest in you slowly changed as he realised you were growing up; I saw the way he looked at you, knew that he wanted you!'

'Then——'

'If I had once acknowledged that I knew of his interest in you, then my marriage would have been at an end!' Janette explained tautly. 'I would have had no other choice, not with my own stepdaughter. So I pretended it had never happened, and you helped to lessen the tension by keeping to your room for the rest of that holiday, and having the good sense never to come back. But Marco never forgot you,' she rasped bitterly. 'When your modelling career took off and your photograph began to appear with sickening regularity in the newspapers I used to see him leering over them, and he would tell anyone willing to listen that you were his beautiful stepdaughter!'

Diana had felt a cold shiver down her spine at the thought of Marco looking at her at all. It was disgusting, obscene, made her feel as if she never wanted her photograph taken ever again.

'I've never hit a woman, Janette,' Reece spoke in slowly measured tones, his face pale, that warning nerve pulsing in his tautly held cheek. 'And I'm certainly not about to soil my hands on you,' he added contemptuously as she instantly looked alarmed. 'So I want you to just tell Diana about Chalford now and then go—before I forget my principles, get over my aversion, and strike you anyway!'

'Let me remind you that I never wanted to be here in the first place,' she glared—but Diana noticed she took a step back away from Reece, just in case!

'Then you shouldn't have come here trying to blackmail Diana,' Reece reminded her harshly.

'I wouldn't have done—if it weren't so damned obvious that there was something odd going on,' Janette scorned. 'If you had known who Diana Lamb was then I would have heard from you, I knew that,' she sneered. 'And if she hadn't told you who she was then there had to be a reason why she hadn't...' She smiled knowingly. 'I suddenly realised exactly what Little Miss Prim was up to.'

'And decided, in your usual devious way——'

'*I* was being devious?' Janette interrupted Reece tauntingly. 'Oh, come on, Reece, you can't blame a girl for——'

'Just get on with it, Janette,' he advised harshly. 'Chalford,' he prompted her bitingly.

She shrugged, turning to Diana. 'Chalford is yours,' she told her in a bored voice. 'It was held in trust for you, meticulously maintained,' she added with a derisive twist of her lip. 'But I was only allowed to stay there if you did, and——'

'Janette!' There was no doubting Reece's almost loss of control now.

She sighed. 'I didn't want to live there anyway, too many damned memories—— OK,' she soothed as Reece looked ready to explode. 'The house is yours, Diana; it became legally yours on your twenty-first birthday.'

It was shock upon shock, upon shock. Diana didn't want to hear that Chalford was hers. Because it made Reece guilty of all she had thought all these years. And she hadn't wanted to know that. Maybe in time, if they had managed to sort out their other problems, she might even have managed to convince herself it had all been a terrible mistake on her part, that Reece couldn't possibly be responsible for those things. She loved him enough to want that to be true. But what she was hearing now made that impossible. And still she loved him...

'Why?' she at last managed to croak.

'Surely that's obvious?' Janette was the one to answer her derisively. 'Poor Howard had shot him——'

'That's enough, Janette!' Reece cut in harshly. 'I can handle this from here.'

'Can you?' Janette scorned, shooting the ashen-faced Diana a pointed look.

He nodded. 'It's all a matter of trust, Janette—something you have no conception of!'

And it was something he and Diana were going to have to learn if they were to have any future together at all. And it was something he knew Diana, green eyes haunted, her face white, a slight tremble to her lips, her hands visibly shaking, wasn't going to find easy to do. He had known how traumatic this was going to be for her, but at the same time he knew it couldn't be delayed any longer.

He looked at Janette again now, instantly struck by the contrast between the two women, Janette so hard and mocking, even in the face of the pain she knew she must be inflicting on Diana—and the anger that would evoke in him!

He shook his head. 'What Howard ever saw in you to take his own life because he knew he had lost you I'll never know,' he said disgustedly, hands thrust deep into his trouser pockets, because at that moment he would dearly have loved to throttle her, and damn the consequences.

'That isn't why he—why he died!' Diana gasped protestingly, her eyes full of the memory now of the horror she would never be able to forget.

'Oh, yes,' Reece said gently, his expression softened with understanding as he well remembered the accusation Howard had thrown at him concerning Janette. But what he also knew, and Diana couldn't, was that it had only been Howard's way of explaining in his own mind why Janette was leaving him; Howard simply hadn't been able to accept the truth—that his wife had no intention of standing by him in the face of financial and social ruin. 'It's exactly the reason he died.' He gave a regretful sigh as Diana seemed to pale even more.

'Howard had got himself involved in a business deal that went sadly wrong, and he persuaded me, much against my better judgement but because he was a friend, to help him out with a loan until things got back on their feet. And he insisted on putting Chalford up as collateral for the loan,' he added grimly. 'I never wanted your home, Diana,' he told her quietly. 'But your father was a man of honour, and when he lost everything else he insisted that a deal was a deal, that Chalford was now mine. And when he told Janette, she gave him the last blow by telling him she had no intention of staying with him when he had no money *and* no house,' he rasped disgustedly. 'Isn't that what happened, Janette?' he prompted hardly. 'There was no affair between us. Ever!'

She avoided his icy gaze and Diana's pained one. 'For God's sake, Reece, it's history——'

'It affects the present,' he grated harshly.

Janette glared at him with hate-filled eyes. 'All right, so I did tell Howard I wasn't going to stand smilingly at his side while our world came crashing down around our ears,' she snapped defensively. 'The other part was his own invention. He knew I found you attractive; can I help it if he chose to draw his own conclusions about my leaving him?' she scorned.

Reece could see the effect all of this was having on Diana, knew she realised exactly why her father had taken his own life now. And her expression was a

mixture of relief and—— He wasn't sure what the
other emotion was. But God, he knew what he hoped
it was!

Diana was barely aware of Reece pointedly holding the
door open for Janette to leave, having difficulty herself taking in all that had been revealed about the past
during the last half-hour. Was it really only half an
hour? But it had changed her whole view of things.
Because she had listened that day as a child, a child
who worshipped her father, had heard his distress and
instantly felt defensive on his behalf, disliking intensely the person causing him anguish and pain.
Reece... She had listened as a child, judged as a child,
felt protective towards her father, as any child would.
    And on her father's part she could see now that, like
any wounded animal, he had turned on anyone who
came near him, the loss of his wife taking away any
reason he might still have had after the blow of financial ruin. Not even the existence of his daughter had
been enough, she now realised, to shake him out of his
despondency, and he certainly hadn't wanted to listen
to Reece when he'd tried to tell him he didn't want his
house or his wife! She didn't doubt that Reece had
wanted to help him that day; she had come to know
the real Reece these last few weeks, and realised now
that, although he could be arrogant, demanding, even
ruthless, he was not a man who enjoyed seeing others
in pain, and he certainly didn't maliciously inflict it.
And he had thought of her father as a friend, he had
said, and, thinking back to that conversation she had
overheard, she realised now that her father had been

the aggressive one, completely unwilling to listen to anything Reece might have to say.

And Janette, the beautiful, selfish Janette, had no reason to lie, had nothing to gain by the things she had admitted. Ultimately, in her selfishness and greed, the other woman had become the loser.

Diana only hoped she and Reece weren't going to be the same, that they could manage to salvage something from this mess. It would be the biggest tragedy of all if they couldn't...

Her eyes swam with unshed tears when she looked across the room at Reece as he stood there so still and wary. 'You know what I believed,' she choked. 'And I'm not even going to attempt to evade admitting my motivation in meeting you. But I want you to know, I fell in love with you anyway, Reece,' she told him almost pleadingly. 'I love you so very much.' If nothing else, she owed him that!

'At last!' he groaned weakly, crossing the room with determined strides to come down on his knees beside her and take her fiercely into his arms. 'God, Diana, you have no idea how frightened I've been,' he rasped. 'How utterly helpless I've felt. Just plain scared!' he admitted shakily before kissing her with an intensity that left them both breathless, Reece cradling each side of her face with tender hands. 'I love you so much that nothing else matters to me. And I do mean nothing,' he said shakily.

Diana clung to him, feeling as if the two of them had been through a hurricane only to emerge together on the other side of it if not exactly on safe ground, at least in calmer waters. 'For years I hated you for what I thought you had done to my family——'

'It would have been unusual if you hadn't, believing what you did,' he comforted.

She shook her head, dazed at her own actions now that she thought back on them. 'I still can't believe what I almost—— It was meeting Chris that had such an impact on me,' she explained shakily, shaking her head. 'Until then I had never realised just how deep-rooted my dislike of the Falcon family was. But there he was, young, successful, never having had to struggle for anything in his life—— I know that isn't completely true now,' she conceded as Reece would have protested. 'But at the time he just seemed like a rather spoilt young man. And he had decided he wanted me. His arrogance seemed——'

'Exactly like mine,' Reece accepted ruefully.

'Yes,' she acknowledged heavily. 'And suddenly all the old resentment and hatred came back, and I couldn't——'

'Darling, you had a right,' Reece told her gently. 'Especially after what you suffered at the hands of Janette and that husband of hers.' A savage light entered his eyes. 'I'd like to break every bone——'

'Marco isn't important, Reece,' she assured him firmly—knowing that he wasn't, that he never really had been. 'It's all over now. I want to get on with living rather than just existing. And I want to do that with you—if you'll have me.' She looked at him with shyly questioning eyes.

His arms moved about her possessively. 'I'm not letting you out of my sight again now that I know you love me!'

Some of the tension left her as she gave a shaky laugh. 'That could be rather awkward for you . . .' she attempted to tease, knowing they had been through so much since they met that they needed the light relief of being able to indulge in a little banter now. Reece, she realised, had lost weight during the last week; he was much leaner, his face looking almost gaunt from the tremendous strain he had been under. And how she *hated* to see him like this; she inwardly made a vow to erase every one of those worry-lines between his eyes with her love.

'Nevertheless, I'm keeping you with me!' he ably demonstrated that his arrogance was back in full force already!

Diana smiled indulgently. 'I don't want to go anywhere.'

'Not even Chalford?' He quirked dark brows. 'It's yours, you know. I never wanted the damned place. I tried, that day, to tell your father that I had only accepted it as collateral because he had insisted, that I didn't want the estate, that I was willing to weather the financial storm with him until things swung back in his favour—as they eventually would have done.'

Reece shook his head. 'I never wanted to take his home away from him, or his family. He had already lost so much, it would have been like kicking a whipped puppy. But Howard didn't want to listen to anything I had to say that day.' His face was as haunted by the memories as Diana's was. 'I decided to leave, come back when things had calmed down a little. Maybe if I had insisted he listen to me that day——'

'Don't, Reece!' She put silencing fingers over his lips. 'The past can't be changed, no matter how much both of us wish for those "maybes". Let it go,' she said softly.

He frowned concernedly. 'Can you?'

'Oh, yes,' she nodded with certainty, knowing she had to let the past go now, that it was her future with Reece that mattered.

'And Chalford?' Reece prompted. 'It's there waiting for you. If you want it.'

She swallowed hard, overwhelmed by the knowledge that the estate had been hers all the time.

Reece scowled. 'I could strangle Janette for the way she——! I should never have entrusted her with that allowance for you, but the truth of the matter is I was ill for a while after your father died, and by the time I felt well enough to deal with any business I had all of my time filled trying to sort out your father's financial muddle. I thought the least Janette could be trusted to do was take care of you.' He frowned. 'Maybe I should have followed up on what Janette was doing with the allowance, checked that it really was being spent on you, but the doctors had told me the best thing for you was to be able to carry on as normal a life as possible, without being confronted by a lot of strangers, especially as seeing me again would only bring that traumatic day vividly back into focus. At the time, I had no idea you had actually been present in the room when I was talking to your father in his study that day; I only realised that from Janette a week ago.' He looked grim.

'If I had known I might have insisted the best thing to do for you was get the truth out in the open. But I let myself be swayed by what the doctors said and Janette led me to believe. And she always told me you were well again, happy in school, that when the time came she would hand Chalford over to you.' He shook his head disgustedly at the lies he had been told.

'Chalford...' Diana repeated softly. 'When you told me just now that it was mine, my first instinct was that I could never go back there.' She frowned. 'But then I realised I was being silly, that I have to go back, if only to lay the ghosts to rest once and for all. But I only want to go back to say goodbye,' she added regretfully. 'After that I would like to sell it. Is that all right with you?'

Reece visibly relaxed. 'Yes,' he agreed huskily. 'If you had wanted to live there, I would have done, but, I have to admit, it wouldn't have been easy. Diana, there's still one thing we haven't discussed,' he said with slow reluctance to introduce what was obviously going to be yet another tense moment between them. He drew in a ragged breath. 'When I came to see you the other day, the morning I found Janette here and realised who you were,' he reminded her at her puzzled frown, 'I came to talk to you about something— important to both of us.'

She frowned at his anxiety, remembering now his urgency that day, and she could feel herself tensing as if for a blow, could tell by the return of his strained expression that he wasn't at all sure how she was going to react to what he was going to tell her.

But nothing he could say now would stop her loving him, absolutely nothing.

Reece saw the determined resolve on her face, and his heart constricted with love for her. She had lost so much, suffered so much for one so young, and he didn't want to be the one to cause her any more pain. But he couldn't deceive her either; that would be unforgivable.

There was only one way to approach this! 'Diana, I told you I didn't want any more children because the truth of the matter is, I believe I'm sterile!' So stark, so cold, so—barren!

She looked stunned by the statement, uncomprehending. 'But—I—there's Chris...?' She frowned her puzzlement.

Reece stood up; he couldn't bear her proximity when he was talking about something that affected them both as deeply as this. There was nothing he would like better than to have a child—children—with Diana, a son or a daughter with her deep green eyes and golden hair. God, he *ached* to have a child with her, but—— 'I had mumps.' He spoke abruptly. 'Several years ago now. I was very ill. The chances are——' he sighed raggedly '—that I'm sterile.'

Diana frowned. 'But you aren't sure? I mean, you've never had tests, anything like that?'

He hated the damned thought of it. At least while he didn't know for certain he could put the idea of it from his mind. And as he had never had any interest before in marrying again it hadn't seemed important... He had tried to ignore the possibility when he'd first asked Diana to marry him, but in the end he had known he had to be completely honest with her.

'I'm willing to do that,' he said tightly. 'For you. If you'll——'

'Mumps...' she spoke slowly. 'Reece, when did you have mumps?'

He shrugged, not seeing the significance of the 'when'—it was the 'perhaps' he was sterile that was important. 'Not long after your father died,' he dismissed. 'That was the illness I mentioned earlier.' He shook his head. 'I spent a couple of days in bed, and then I had to get up—I couldn't leave your father's financial affairs any longer. Maybe if I hadn't felt so ill I would have known to pay more attention to your welfare, but I don't think I was thinking very well at all at the time, with a temperature of a hundred and three!'

For a moment Diana just stared at him, and then she nodded slowly. 'I know.' She gave a choked laugh. 'I really do know, Reece.' She stood up to come over to him as he frowned at her reaction. 'The reason I was at home when my father died was because I had been sent home from school because I was ill. If you remember, it was actually term-time. But I had mumps——'

'Mumps?' Reece spoke at the same time she did, having realised exactly what she was trying to tell him. *She* had been the reason he had got the childhood ailment. He had never been able to fathom out where it had come from, since he had known it wasn't from Chris, who had had it years before. It was incredible that it should have been Diana all the time!

'You aren't going to be sterile, Reece,' she told him with determined certainty now. 'The fates couldn't be that cruel to us after all that we've already gone through.'

He looked down at her, his arms about her as he tightly enfolded her to him. 'And if they are?' He had to give her one last chance to change her mind about marrying him, no matter what it cost him. And it would cost him dearly.

She gave him a bright, unshadowed smile. 'Then we have each other, and it won't matter.'

No, it wouldn't; he could see that from her radiantly serene expression. It really wouldn't matter!

What a breath-catching future he had ahead of him, loving, and being loved by, this lovely woman for the rest of his life . . .

EPILOGUE

'DIANA? Diana!'

She woke languidly to the sound of her husband's voice as it rose slightly in agitation, and she stretched slowly, smiling to herself as she remembered the reason she was feeling so sleepy: Reece had woken her early this morning with a passionate intensity that had left them both breathless. It would have been nice if they could have taken a nap together then, but the events of the day had taken over, and it had been mid-morning before she finally found a few minutes to relax in the sitting-room of the beautiful country house they had bought in Berkshire, only to have actually drifted off to sleep, she now realised.

And she didn't need two guesses at what had thrown Reece into this minor panic—she knew it *could* only be one of two things.

'Ah, there you are,' he said with obvious relief as she appeared, slightly tousled, in the sitting-room doorway. 'Help!' He stood in the middle of the hallway looking completely at a loss.

Diana couldn't hold back her indulgent smile, moving gracefully forward to relieve him of one of the shawl-wrapped bundles he held in his arms. 'Sterile, indeed!' she mocked teasingly as she took first one daughter in her arms and then the other, both of them crying for their food now, which was obviously the reason why Reece was looking so helplessly harassed. One baby he could deal with, but their twin daughters contrarily designed to want to do everything at the same time. And poor Reece, so capable and ordered when it came to business, was always at a complete loss to know what to do with them.

'You omitted to mention that your grandmother was a twin,' Reece reminded her as he sat down to watch the rapt expression on his daughters' faces as they latched on to their mother for their milk, almost as much pleasure on his face as he gazed at them with tender love.

'You were sterile, remember, so I didn't think it was important you should know.' She smiled at him indulgently over to the top of two silky blonde heads, absently stroking their legs.

She could still remember the exquisite happiness of knowing she and Reece were to have a child of their own after all, and still chuckled softly to herself every time she thought of Reece's face the night she went into labour and not one baby was born to them but two, both girls, and completely identical. Nothing of twins had shown up on the scan she had had, and so they had only been expecting the one baby. But she loved Alexandra and Victoria with a fierceness she knew Reece echoed—for all they threw him into a panic every now and then!

'Thank God I became a father again before I'm presented with my grandchild!' Reece said now with feeling.

'Only just,' Diana laughed softly. 'Maddy's baby is due in three weeks' time.' And Chris and Maddy's marriage, for all the relationship had had a few rocky patches, was a happy one, the young couple ecstatic at the thought of their own child, and Chris almost as shocked as his father at the birth of twin sisters!

'As long as they don't have twins too,' Reece grinned, still a little dazed by his two daughters, even though the babies were two months old now.

But Diana had no doubts that these two little imps in her arms were going to twist their wonderful father around their tiny little fingers as they grew up, and that Reece would lavish as much love on them as he did on her.

Happiness, as Diana knew only too well, was loving and being loved by this man.

POSTCARDS FROM EUROPE

HARLEQUIN PRESENTS®

Hi—

The sun was shining brightly here in Spain *until* I met Felipe de Santis. The man is used to giving orders and doesn't respect my abilities as a journalist. But I'm going to get my story—and I'm going to help Felipe's sister!

Love, Maggie

P.S. If only I could win Felipe's love....

Travel across Europe in 1994 with Harlequin Presents. Collect a new *Postcards From Europe* title each month!

Don't miss
DARK SUNLIGHT
by Patricia Wilson
Harlequin Presents #1644

Available in April, wherever Harlequin Presents books are sold.

HPPFE4

Relive the romance. . .
Harlequin and Silhouette are proud to present

A program of collections of three complete novels by the most
requested authors with the most requested themes.

Available in April:

MEN IN UNIFORM

No one can resist them!

Three complete novels in one special collection:

NAVY BLUES by Debbie Macomber
RED TAIL by Lindsay McKenna
DEMON LOVER by Kathleen Creighton

Available wherever ❤ *Silhouette* ®

books are sold.

SREQ494

HARLEQUIN®

PRESENTS Plus

Meet Kieran Sinclair. He believes Tegan heartlessly
jilted his wheelchair-bound friend and now he's
determined to exact revenge—in the form of her
pagan surrender.

And then there's Jerome Moncourt. When Meg
accidentally falls into his arms, she discovers that she
isn't the only one participating in a dangerous charade.
The handsome Frenchman has his own secrets!

Kieran and Jerome are just two of the sexy men you'll
fall in love with each month in Harlequin Presents Plus.

Watch for
Pagan Surrender by Robyn Donald
Harlequin Presents Plus #1639

and

Dawn Song by Sara Craven
Harlequin Presents Plus #1640

Harlequin Presents Plus
The best has just gotten better!

Available in April, wherever Harlequin books are sold.

PPLUS11

Fifty red-blooded, white-hot, true-blue hunks
from every State in the Union!

Look for MEN MADE IN AMERICA! Written by some
of our most poplar authors, these stories feature fifty of
the strongest, sexiest men, each from a different state in
the union!

Two titles available every other month at your favorite
retail outlet.

In March, look for:

TANGLED LIES by Anne Stuart (Hawaii)
ROGUE'S VALLEY by Kathleen Creighton (Idaho)

In May, look for:

LOVE BY PROXY by Diana Palmer (Illinois)
POSSIBLES by Lass Small (Indiana)

You won't be able to resist MEN MADE IN AMERICA!

If you missed your state or would like to order any other states that have already been published, send your name, address, zip or postal code along with a check or money order (please
do not send cash) for $3.59 for each book, plus 75¢ postage and handling ($1.00 in Canada),
payable to Harlequin Reader Service, to:

In the U.S.

3010 Walden Avenue
P.O. Box 1369
Buffalo, NY 14269-1369

In Canada

P.O. Box 609
Fort Erie, Ontario
L2A 5X3

Please specify book title(s) with your order.
Canadian residents add applicable federal and provincial taxes.

MEN394

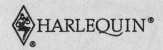

HARLEQUIN®

MARRIAGE BY Design

Harlequin proudly presents four stories about *convenient* but not *conventional* reasons for marriage:

- ◆ To save your godchildren from a "wicked stepmother"

- ◆ To help out your eccentric aunt — and her sexy business partner

- ◆ To bring an old man happiness by making him a grandfather

- ◆ To escape from a ghostly existence and become a real woman

Marriage By Design — four brand-new stories by four of Harlequin's most popular authors:

CATHY GILLEN THACKER
JASMINE CRESSWELL
GLENDA SANDERS
MARGARET CHITTENDEN

Don't miss this exciting collection of stories about marriages of convenience. Available in April, wherever Harlequin books are sold.

MBD94

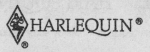

HARLEQUIN®

COMING SOON TO
A STORE NEAR YOU...

THE MAIN
ATTRACTION

By *New York Times* Bestselling Author

This March, look for THE MAIN ATTRACTION by popular
author Jayne Ann Krentz.

Ten years ago, Filomena Cromwell had left her small town
in shame. Now she is back determined to get her sweet,
sweet revenge....

Soon she has her ex-fiancé, who cheated on her with
another woman, chasing her all over town. And he isn't
the only one. Filomena lets Trent Ravinder catch her.

Can she control the fireworks she's set into motion?

BOB8

HARLEQUIN®

Don't miss these Harlequin favorites by some of our most distinguished authors!
And now, you can receive a discount by ordering two or more titles!

HT#25409	THE NIGHT IN SHINING ARMOR by JoAnn Ross	$2.99	☐
HT#25471	LOVESTORM by JoAnn Ross	$2.99	☐
HP#11463	THE WEDDING by Emma Darcy	$2.89	☐
HP#11592	THE LAST GRAND PASSION by Emma Darcy	$2.99	☐
HR#03188	DOUBLY DELICIOUS by Emma Goldrick	$2.89	☐
HR#03248	SAFE IN MY HEART by Leigh Michaels	$2.89	☐
HS#70464	CHILDREN OF THE HEART by Sally Garrett	$3.25	☐
HS#70524	STRING OF MIRACLES by Sally Garrett	$3.39	☐
HS#70500	THE SILENCE OF MIDNIGHT by Karen Young	$3.39	☐
HI#22178	SCHOOL FOR SPIES by Vickie York	$2.79	☐
HI#22212	DANGEROUS VINTAGE by Laura Pender	$2.89	☐
HI#22219	TORCH JOB by Patricia Rosemoor	$2.89	☐
HAR#16459	MACKENZIE'S BABY by Anne McAllister	$3.39	☐
HAR#16466	A COWBOY FOR CHRISTMAS by Anne McAllister	$3.39	☐
HAR#16462	THE PIRATE AND HIS LADY by Margaret St. George	$3.39	☐
HAR#16477	THE LAST REAL MAN by Rebecca Flanders	$3.39	☐
HH#28704	A CORNER OF HEAVEN by Theresa Michaels	$3.99	☐
HH#28707	LIGHT ON THE MOUNTAIN by Maura Seger	$3.99	☐

Harlequin Promotional Titles

#83247	YESTERDAY COMES TOMORROW by Rebecca Flanders	$4.99	☐
#83257	MY VALENTINE 1993	$4.99	☐
	(short-story collection featuring Anne Stuart, Judith Arnold, Anne McAllister, Linda Randall Wisdom)		

(limited quantities available on certain titles)

	AMOUNT	$
DEDUCT:	10% DISCOUNT FOR 2+ BOOKS	$
ADD:	POSTAGE & HANDLING	$
	($1.00 for one book, 50¢ for each additional)	
	APPLICABLE TAXES*	$ _____
	TOTAL PAYABLE	$ _____
	(check or money order—please do not send cash)	

To order, complete this form and send it, along with a check or money order for the total above, payable to Harlequin Books, to: **In the U.S.:** 3010 Walden Avenue, P.O. Box 9047, Buffalo, NY 14269-9047; **In Canada:** P.O. Box 613, Fort Erie, Ontario, L2A 5X3.

Name: _____

Address: _____ City: _____

State/Prov.: _____ Zip/Postal Code: _____

*New York residents remit applicable sales taxes.
 Canadian residents remit applicable GST and provincial taxes.

HBACK-JM